Reclaiming Charity

Shaped by Love

By

USA *Today* BESTSELLING AUTHOR

MARION UECKERMANN

Contact Information: marion.ueckermann@gmail.com

Cover Art by Marion Ueckermann: www.marionueckermann.net

Edited by Ailsa Williams.

Cover Image ID 113675052 purchased from Depositphotos © Subbotina
Sunflower ID 33819345 purchased from Depositphotos © Ksena32

ISBN: 9781095736630

PRAISE FOR *Reclaiming Charity*

Sparks fly in Marion Ueckermann's novel, *Reclaiming Charity*, a book that keeps you guessing from start to finish. With real-life characters and attention-grabbing situations, as well as some good old fashioned mid-west charm, the plot rolls along to a satisfying conclusion. Not to be missed!

~ Jan Elder, Author of the Creek Series

This story really tugs at the heartstrings. There is a great sense of relief when the only thing that could ever give Brody a sense of being loved and accepted comes to him via his sister. There is hope for the Brody's of this world!

~ Ailsa Williams, Editor

This is a true masterpiece, woven with threads of grace, forgiveness, trust, enduring faith, and God's relentless love towards us! It tackles the difficult and deep issues of fear, rejection, abandonment, and feelings of being unworthy of God's love. Deeply moving, with broad strokes of trusting in the skill of the Master to finish the canvas of our lives, and brushed with the gold thread of hope that He will truly remake the messy situations into a good and beautiful picture. With the stroke of her pen, Marion has created another masterpiece, where Charity may indeed be the greatest!

~ Becky Smith

I really love the quote at the beginning of this book: "Some artworks appear chaotic, but it all depends on the eye of the beholder." Chaotic is what Charity felt her life was. Her parents appeared to be creative loving people, but sometimes that creative spirit leads to chaos. If it wasn't for Charity's faith and hope in God, plus her prayer journals, she might not make it.

This book deals with trust and faith issues, as well as, marital and family dynamics. These are all major issues which are currently creating havoc in our society. Marion Ueckermann is a very gifted author and she has taken these issues and woven a beautiful story of healing. She also paints a touching story of how God can take the blank or messed-up canvas of our life and turn it into a masterpiece.

I highly recommend you read this book because I know it will touch your heart!

~ Marylin Furumasu, MF Literary Works

A compelling inspiring story about Faith's (*Restoring Faith–Book 1*) brother Brody being transformed by the Master Artist. Marion Ueckermann's well crafted, emotional story has this avid reader coming back for another page turning read. The reader is immediately drawn into Brody and Madison's marital discord which evokes sympathy for their teen daughter Charity, who daily pours out her heart in a prayer journal. Imagery has the reader visualizing the beauty of Cottonwood Falls, the art scene in New York City, unique paintings, dazzling fashion, and scrumptious cuisine. Foreshadowing alludes to the cause of Brody's deep rooted issue of anger, turmoil, and abandonment. Life can be messy and some artwork appears chaotic; but the Lord, the Master Painter, can make everything beautiful in its time.

~ Renate Pennington, Retired English, Journalism, Creative Writing High School Teacher

Marion Ueckermann has written another must read! When a

character is so well written that I simply want to grab hold and shake them, well that's a winner in my book!

We can all let life and past hurts get in the way of God's best for us, but when Brody has kept a secret for so long that it threatens the very people he loves most in the world, he is faced with a choice.

Madison has a charmed life with her husband and daughter, if only she and Brody didn't argue all the time...ah, but making up?!

Charity is the sweetest of 16 year olds who loves God and her parents with her whole heart. I loved every moment of this beautiful journey!

~ Paula Marie, Blogger and Book Reviewer at Fiction Full of Faith

Reclaiming Charity by Marion Ueckermann is a marvelous contemporary Christian novel. Within the novel there is a marriage in trouble. Marion Ueckermann pulls no punches. She shows the ups and downs of a relationship which has very high highs and very low lows. The fallout reaches a teenage daughter who at times seems wiser than her parents. The reader feels her pain as she would hate to have to choose between them.

Once again Marion Ueckermann has created characters that are easy to identify with. They are not perfect but realistically flawed. Marion Ueckermann does not present us with fairy tales but with stories of gritty issues that may affect us. She shows that life is not always smooth but that God is always faithful.

~ Julia Wilson, Book Reviewer at Christian Bookaholic

Early wounds leave deep scars on our children. Sometimes they curse the next generation as well. Marion Ueckermann weaves a masterful story of hurt and healing, demonstrating anything is possible with God, even the healing of deep wounds and keloid scars. This is the final story in her planned Potter's House series.

But there is one more story to be told. I look forward to convincing her to write an epilogue novella.

~ Judith Robl, JR's Red Quill Editing, Author of *As Grandma Says*

This was awesome, amazing book full of laughter, tears, and most of all God's love, forgiveness and redemption. The best part of the book was reading Charity's prayer journal. I highly recommend this book to those who love Christian fiction with a strong inspirational message.

~ Linda Rainey

A story that came close to my heart as I resonated with Madison and Brody in so many ways. Marriage is most precious, but it's hard work. Learning to overcome the ups and downs is a valuable lesson of marriage that Marion has taught so well through this story. A page turner that reflects on God's love, mercy and grace for us all.

~ Sharon Dean

Dear Reader

Life can be messy,
not a pretty picture at all.
Sometimes the erratic scribbles of existence
can make you feel more Picasso than Picot.
Stay firmly fixed to the Master's easel
because God is not finished
painting your portrait.
And never, ever forget that you are
His masterpiece!

Be blessed,

For Karen ~

A Masterpiece in the galleries of heaven.
We will always miss you.

For Karen ~

A Masterpiece in the galleries of heaven.
We will always miss you.

What God has joined together,
let no one separate.

~ Mark 10:9 (NIV)

CHAPTER ONE

Wednesday, June 8, 2005

ARTISTS ARE recluses, Madison Peterson's husband, Brody, often joked, but their move to the tiny town of Cottonwood Falls had offered their daughter a slower, safer, more innocent way of life. Madison had to admit that despite growing up in the fast lane—a New York socialite for a mother and her father a Wall Street banker—like Brody, she herself was somewhat of a recluse. She didn't like crowds. Their handful of friends suited her just fine.

Then again, she was an artist too.

At first, the transition had been tough for Madison—she'd been used to a faster paced life—but as the years rolled into each other, she grew to love living in rural Kansas. Now, she wouldn't trade it for anything. The wide-open spaces, the Flint Hills where fields sloped gently this way and that, and the stars that shone brighter in the heavens. Not to mention all the great venues not too far in any direction for the artist to seek out. It would take a *lot* to drag her away.

"Not much longer, Charity honey. I promise." Standing at the edge of their backyard overlooking farmer Thorpe's wheat field, Madison dipped the number two Winsor & Newton round brush—perfect for the finer features of her daughter's face—into the blob of rose madder tint she'd squeezed onto her palette. She mixed it with a touch of white. Perfect. Exactly the right color for Charity's rosebud lips.

Humming softly, Madison swirled the sturdy hog bristles in the oil paint, then lifted the brush. Charity's beautiful face smiled from the large canvas as she reached for a bright yellow sunflower in a field of gold, her long, reddish curls blowing gently in the afternoon breeze. *Wow! I could not have chosen a better pose or setting for this piece of art. And right here in our own backyard.* With the sun's rays falling on Charity's white cotton dress, the painting radiated summer, which, thankfully, was nearly here.

Even though the fields were green, not quite ripe for harvest, when she'd put the first dabs of oil to the canvas, Madison had opted to paint them in the golds of harvest time now before her eyes. The sunflower, too, was an adjustment she'd made to the actual visual she painted from—the tinier wild sunflowers that graced the Kansas roadsides throughout summer not yet in bloom when she'd started the artwork.

Madison released a satisfied sigh at her handiwork. She'd been busy with this portrait for weeks now, a birthday gift for her baby, and she was almost done. In the nick of time too. The paint would barely have sufficient time to dry after she added the final brushstrokes today.

Sweet sixteen next Saturday—how had that happened? In a blink, Charity had morphed from a babe in diapers to the beautiful young woman standing in the field behind their home. There was no doubt in Madison's mind this sweet sixteen would arrive with a never been kissed. Oh the sweetness of Charity's innocence—long may it last.

A smile tugged. Madison felt sorry for the boy who *did* try to kiss her daughter one day. Charity was as pure as they came—her heart belonged to Jesus, she always said. And for that, neither Brody nor Madison could take credit. That was all Faith's doing. From the time Charity had given her life to God at the tender age of eight during a visit to Brody's sister in Colorado, Charity had insisted on going to Sunday school every Sunday morning— whether her parents came to church with her or not.

Madison and Brody went on the odd occasion, but not often. They just weren't…church people. Besides, they did some of their best work on the weekends. So while Charity was learning about Jesus, they'd busy themselves packing paints, canvases, and easels into the SUV, ready to head on out the moment Charity emerged from Sunday school.

Some days Madison envied her daughter. Charity had an inner peace that neither she nor Brody had been able to find.

As did Faith and Brody's younger brother, Tyler. There was just something different about them. These Christians.

Maybe sometime she'd need to give this church stuff more of a chance.

Still, Madison couldn't help wondering whether Charity would've turned out so perfect, so unblemished, had they stayed in New York. Could her faith have protected her as much in the city?

Perhaps there was method in her husband's madness in moving them from the Big Apple to live in this sleepy hollow.

Charity's laugh drew Madison's attention from the artwork. She looked up from behind the easel in time to see her daughter lose her pose as she toppled sideways.

"Honey, you need to stand still."

Charity righted herself, scrunching her nose. "I'm trying, Mom. It's Baxter. He's jumping up and tugging at my dress."

Madison lowered her gaze to see a flash of cream between the sheaths of wheat.

"Baxt—? How did that dog sneak out of the house?" Madison pursed her lips. She was beginning to think that giving in to Charity's pleas to get a puppy for her birthday had perhaps not been the wisest decision she and Brody had made. But the Golden Retriever pup was sooo cute, even she couldn't resist him.

The bouncy early birthday present and the painting weren't the only gifts they'd planned for Charity. Their daughter knew about the artwork—obviously, as she was posing for it—but Charity wouldn't see it until her party. Madison wasn't sure if she was more excited to see the look on Charity's face when they unveiled the canvas or when they handed over the keys to the spanking new VW Beetle—new-shape—the color of Dorothy's brick road in the Land of Oz.

They had wanted to buy her something less expensive, second-hand, but Grandpa Harding-Forbes had insisted his granddaughter drive a brand new, trendier car—after all, in another year she'd be going to college and would need something reliable to commute home on weekends and breaks. The next morning Madison received a call from the dealership in Emporia to inform her that a yellow Beetle had been ordered for Charity Peterson by a James Harding-Forbes with a fifty percent down payment paid.

Madison shook her head. Her father and mother always seemed to get their way.

"Take him back inside, Charity, and lock him in your room this time so he can't get out. We'll only be another hour or so. He'll be fine."

While Charity returned Baxter to the confines of the house, Madison added a few touches of raw sienna and cadmium yellow to the background.

With Baxter safely secured in her bedroom, Charity returned to pose in the field, and Madison continued to immortalize her daughter in a landscape of Kansas sunshine.

By the time Brody returned from their gallery in Emporia, the sun had inched its way closer to the horizon. Charity had just returned to her room to give poor Baxter some TLC. Only a few more touches and Madison could call it a night.

Madison started as Brody wrapped his arms around her waist, narrowly missing adding an unwanted streak of blue across the sunflower.

"Babe, *that* is Kansas on a canvas." He chuckled. "Bit of a tongue-twister."

Nuzzling her neck, his breath warm against her ear, he whispered, "Incredible. That has to be your best piece ever."

"Ha, you're only saying that because you're biased." Madison twisted around and stroked the brush down Brody's nose, leaving a thin blue line on the chiseled bridge.

Brody's brows lifted. "Biased? How can I not be when that's my baby girl there, painted by the delicate hands of my very, very talented one true love?"

A soft laugh escaped past Madison's lips as she greeted him with a light kiss. She smoothed her free hand over his five o'clock shadow then moved her fingers to the nape of his neck to loosen the band holding his hair back in a short ponytail. Soft brown waves spilled onto his collar, and Madison noticed that the tailored jacket he had left with that morning had been discarded. As usual. Brody hated having to dress up for the gallery. Give him a pair of jeans and a T-shirt and he was happy.

She smiled. "Time to let your hair down, my love."

"It is. It's been a pretty hectic day." He drew her into a deeper kiss, no doubt transferring that blue paint to her cheek. Resting his forehead against hers, Brody's ice-blue gaze searched hers. His voice husky, he mumbled, "I missed you at the gallery today."

Her heart swelled. How she adored this man, even though at

times he could be quite difficult.

Then again, so could she.

Both blamed it on the artist's emotive temperament.

Emotive? More like explosive.

A slow smile curved her lips. "And I missed being there. Thank you for giving me the time these past few weeks to finish this piece." Normally, Madison accompanied Brody to the gallery every Wednesday. This was the fourth week in a row that she hadn't. While he curated the gallery with the help of his assistant, Ava, Madison churned out completed canvases—commissioned works plus the odd piece for sale to display in the gallery.

"It was for an important cause." Brody gazed past Madison and his eyes narrowed as he scrutinized the canvas behind her. "You done?"

Madison turned around, admiring the portrait with more satisfaction than she'd done with anything else she'd painted. "I am. Finally."

"And she hasn't seen it?"

Madison shook her head. "Gives the canvas a wide berth every time she passes. She knows better. She's a good girl."

"The best." Brody reached for the painting, his fingers carefully clasping the canvas frame at the sides. He lifted it off the French easel. "I'll take this inside to the studio."

He turned to go then paused. "Oh, I got Chinese takeout. I figured you wouldn't have time to make dinner."

"You're the best." Madison stretched to plant a quick kiss on Brody's cheek before focusing her attention on packing up the easel—paint supplies and palette into the sketchbox first, then collapsing the legs and canvas arm. With everything neatly folding into one smaller package, a must for the traveling artist, she'd be ready to join Brody in no time.

And dig into that Chinese food. Her favorite.

She lifted her gaze to watch Brody make his way across the lawn.

"Baxter! Come back here." Charity burst from the house chasing after the pup that flatly ignored her.

Oh no...

Madison dropped the easel and shouted, "Charity, get back inside. Now! And take that dog with you." The last thing she needed was Brody tripping over a ball of cream fur, her not-so-dry painting crashing onto the grass.

Not to mention their daughter seeing the work of art they'd carefully managed to hide. Until now.

Charity skidded to a stop, hand in front of her face. "I didn't see anything. I promise."

Baxter continued on with not a care in the world. Tail wagging like a metronome set to *prestissimo*, the pooch was beyond excited to be outside once again.

Not for long.

"Baxter!" Madison rushed forward to block the pup's path.

The Golden Retriever zig-zagged then double-backed toward Charity. As he neared her, Charity lunged and grabbed the puppy by the base of the tail. A loud yelp erupted before Baxter curled into Charity's embrace.

"I got him!" she shouted, her voice triumphant.

As Charity shoved to her feet, dusting off her dress, Madison took one look and groaned. Would she ever get that grass stain out of the white cotton?

"Charity! Close your eyes." The back of the canvas facing their daughter, Brody slipped past Charity and up the porch steps. He disappeared inside the house.

Phew. That was close.

Baxter squirmed in Charity's arms, eager to be on his feet, running in the yard.

7

Eyes still shut tightly, Charity hefted him a little higher.

Defeated, the pup settled his chin on her shoulder.

"Charity honey, you can open your eyes now," Madison said.

Charity's eyes fluttered open, brimming with regret as she fixed her gaze on Madison. "I'm so sorry, Mom. I probably didn't shut the bedroom door properly. Next thing I knew, he was headed for the back door." Her gaze shifted to the easel and tubes of paint scattered on the grass. "Is there anything I can help with?"

"I got this, honey. But maybe in a minute or so you can heat up the takeout Dad got in town? I'll be along shortly." Madison returned to the easel she'd discarded on the grass and the paints that had fallen out of the sketchbox.

With her art supplies safely stored in the home studio, Madison joined Charity and Brody where they sat waiting at the kitchen table. Charity had already changed out of the dress and into a pair of jeans and a T-shirt. Charity wasn't a fan of dresses. It had taken a lot of arguments, eye-rolls, and because-I-say-so's to get her daughter to agree on wearing the one they'd finally chosen for her party next Saturday. But Madison had to make sure the party was up to her mother's high standards—well, as high as she could get it in Cottonwood Falls. And yes, especially Charity's outfit. Her parents had insisted they weren't missing their only granddaughter's sixteenth birthday and planned to fly in from New York for the afternoon on the company's nine-seater jet.

Charity looked up at Madison and smiled. "Perfect timing, Mom. I've just taken the paper pails out of the microwave."

"Thank you, sweetheart." Madison sank into her chair, exhausted, and reached for a container. General Tso's Chicken with fried rice. Yum. That was enough to peak her flagging energy levels.

She unwrapped a pair of chopsticks.

Brody and Charity grabbed their food too.

Charity was about to sink the long bamboo sticks into her meal when she stopped. "Mom, is that blue paint on your cheek?"

Madison rubbed at her cheek where Brody's painted nose had pressed against her skin. "Probably."

Lips pressed in a thin line, a smirk hiding unsuccessfully behind it, Charity tipped her chin. "Right... I think Dad had a smudged line of exactly the same blue paint down his nose. I wonder how he got it. And you."

Brody's deep laugh circled the room. "Yeah, I wonder."

Madison pointed a chopstick in their direction. "You two, eat your food."

"So, baby girl, are you ready to take your driver's license test? Only two more weeks..." Brody leaned his head back and dropped a piece of the sweet and spicy chicken into his mouth.

Beside him, Baxter whined as he watched Brody clamp another juicy piece of chicken between the sticks.

Charity's head bobbed up and down. "I am, and I can't wait."

She leaned over and patted Baxter's head. "That'll make you ill. Only puppy food for you, I'm afraid. Besides, you're just being greedy now—you've already eaten."

Baxter dipped his head to the side in a sway and yapped.

Everyone burst into laughter.

Turning her attention back to Brody, Charity folded her arms on the table. "So, Dad, does that mean I'm getting a car for my sixteenth birthday? Seeing as you insisted I first complete a driver education course."

Charity could have taken her license at fifteen, but Madison and Brody were reluctant to let their daughter grow up too fast. As Charity was only applying for her GDL at sixteen, she actually didn't need to take the driver education course, but they'd both agreed they wanted Charity to know how to drive *before* she got her permit.

Brody feigned surprise. "Ha, a car? You just got a dog for your birthday."

Charity leaned forward and melted onto her arms. Chin resting on her forearms, she looked up, the same puppy eyes as Baxter's flitting between Madison and Brody. "I can't drive a dog... It wouldn't need to be anything fancy; just something to get me around."

She heaved a sigh then pushed herself upright again and returned to her meal. "Anyway, I just thought I'd mention it...in case the idea hadn't crossed your mind and you were stumped as to what to get me for my birthday."

Madison ran her tongue over her teeth to hide her smile. Their daughter knew just how to wrap her dad around her little finger. Little did she know she'd already managed to get her wish without even trying.

"Eat up, honey, before your food gets cold." Rising from her chair, Madison clasped her and Brody's empty containers between her fingers. She walked over to the trash can and disposed of them. "I'm going to take a quick shower. After all, I do have blue paint on my face to get rid of."

Brody's chair scraped against the floor as he hurried to his feet, a mischievous grin on his face. "So do I. Think I should clean up too."

After they'd all taken showers, Madison's stretching a little longer than she'd anticipated because she'd had company, they plunked down on the sofa in front of the TV to enjoy some family time. If only life could always be this peaceful in their home. Madison hated it when she and Brody fought.

Charity hated it more. Her daughter never said it, but a mother knew.

When they'd watched a few of their favorite sitcoms, Charity carefully rose from her seat, a sleepy puppy cradled in her arms.

Already, those two were inseparable. "Night, Mom and Dad. I'm going to bed."

"Night, sweetheart," Brody and Madison echoed.

Giving a lengthy yawn, Brody inched his way off the couch. "I'm heading upstairs as well. You coming?"

Madison looked up at him. She reached for his hand and squeezed it. "In a minute, love. I need to answer a few emails, and then I'll join you."

"Don't be long." Brody's roguish smile made her anxious to join her husband, but she had something she needed to do first.

Something important.

Something that could be life-changing.

Once she was certain Brody was safely upstairs, Madison tiptoed down the passage into their office just off the studio. She turned on her laptop and sank into her chair.

She pulled up the webpage of her favorite online art magazine, *Art-e-Fact*. She loved browsing through the site. So many interesting ideas and events. And one of those events had recently caught her eye.

Art USA.

The contest called for entries in all mediums—acrylic, oil, watercolor, pencil, chalk, photography, sculpture, bas-relief… You name it. If it was art, it could be entered. The only rule—the artwork must epitomize the artist's home state where he or she currently resides. In the first round of the contest, a finalist from each state would be chosen, and from there, a first, second, and third winner would represent the best of American art.

Madison stared at the page for the umpteenth time since she'd first seen it a few days ago. It wasn't the fifty thousand dollar prize money that had caught her attention though, it was the opportunity for an exclusive exhibition of the winner's work at one of the most renowned galleries in New York City—Ellie Sanders. A Kansas girl, maybe the great Ellie would be predisposed to entries from her home state.

That could really put Peterson Galleries on the map. And Madison's best friend, Sandy, agreed.

But would Brody allow her to enter? When it came to her artwork, his decisions sometimes seemed…shortsighted. But as curator of their gallery, Brody always had the final say. What if this was one of those times, however, when what he decided didn't make sense and she lost out on an incredible opportunity? She could always enter and apologize later for going over his head if she actually got anywhere in the contest.

Dear Jesus,

How I love this prayer journal idea Aunt Faith started three years ago. Writing something to You every night is the thing I look forward to most at the end of my day (or most days because sometimes I get tired and forget, but I know You don't mind, because You love me). I hope she sends another journal for my birthday, like she has every year, because this one is almost full.

I wish every day at home could be filled with as much love and fun as tonight. I hate it when Mom and Dad argue. That's the reason I gave up painting, because if that's what artists eventually become—irrational, jealous, possessive, unreasonable, and inflexible people—then thanks, but no thanks. I'll take a different talent if You don't mind giving me one.

Please, please let Mom and Dad always be this loving toward each other. Please help them to not fight.

With love
Charity

(Daughter of the Most High God)
(and Brody and Madison Peterson)

P.S. Thank You so much for Baxter. Again. Yes, Mom and Dad gave him to me, but I know You arranged that. I love him so much. He's a bundle of fun.

CHAPTER TWO

WHILE BRODY entertained Charity for the morning in Emporia, Madison rushed around trying to get everything ready for Charity's party at noon. Not an easy feat with a puppy under foot in the kitchen, but she couldn't leave Baxter locked in a room all morning. Especially as he'd have to spend the afternoon there too.

Eventually, Madison could take it no longer. Something had to be done, and outside on his own wasn't an option yet.

"Come, puppy. It's the upstairs bathroom for you." She stooped and lifted Baxter into her arms. She stroked his fur, and in turn, Baxter licked her hand.

Several times.

"Oh, you are so cute, but it's not going to help giving me those soft puppy eyes. I need to get done, and you are a big distraction." Madison hugged him to her chest.

Big mistake.

That puppy breath just melted her heart.

No… Work. Birthday party.

Wrapping her fingers around Baxter's button nose, she shook it gently from side to side. "And you're getting time out until your mistress gets home."

Baxter let out a soft growl then a bark as he nipped playfully at Madison's fingers.

Madison opted to shut Baxter in her and Brody's en suite bathroom instead of Charity's. If any guest needed to use the upstairs facilities, she didn't want the bathroom to smell of puppy poop. And there were bound to be accidents to clean up when she returned. Only two months old, Baxter was far from house-trained.

As she closed the bathroom door, Baxter rushed for the gap, getting his snout wedged in the narrow opening. Two black eyes peered up at her longingly, while the small, wet button nose sniffed the air.

Lowering herself, Madison squatted in front of the door. "Stay, Baxter. It won't be for very long. And please, please, try not to make too much of a mess." Reaching up, she wrapped her fingers around the door handle then gently pushed on the pup's chest until the door was free. She hurried to close the gap.

As she walked away, Baxter began to howl and wail and scratch at the door.

Oh, I hope that paintwork can stand the Baxter test.

With the kitchen finally cleaned up after a morning of baking and cooking, Madison set out the last of the food platters on the perfectly decorated dining room table—shades of pink and brown to match the embellishments on the three-tier cake just delivered by the bakery in Emporia.

How she would've loved to have hosted the party outside, but with the weather forecasting stronger winds today, she'd decided to rather hold the party indoors. The last thing they needed was everything blowing over or away. Guests would soon get irked at having their clothes and hair blown this way and that. Besides, Charity's dress would never stay down if it got blustery. The wisest choice in Kansas was not to chance the weather. Thankfully they had this wonderfully large combined formal living and dining room where their twenty guests could comfortably enjoy the afternoon together without feeling that the space was in the least bit cramped.

Leaning against the wall at the wide entrance to the living room, Madison surveyed her handiwork. Her gaze came to rest on the towering, sweet masterpiece standing on a smaller table in the corner of the dining room. The red velvet birthday cake covered in white fondant was decorated with pink hearts in different shades on the large bottom tier, pink and brown vertical stripes on the middle cake, and polka dots in the same two colors on the small top layer. Edible pink peonies finished the culinary work of art. And although magnificent, Madison suddenly wondered at the wisdom in her choice of three layers. Unless she sent her guests home with chunks of the sweet stuff, the three of them were going to be eating cake for days.

Overhead, triangular party flags, the color of the cake's embellishments, zigzagged the ceiling—both the length and the breadth of the room.

Madison glanced up at the wall clock. Eleven a.m. She only had an hour to get ready before their guests started arriving.

Angst tightened her gut. What was keeping Brody and Charity? They were cutting it fine—they both needed to get ready for the party too.

And Charity was the guest of honor.

About to head upstairs for a shower, Madison suddenly remembered. *The painting.* She'd almost forgotten to put it on display.

She hurried to the studio and grabbed her finest easel. After setting it up in one corner of the living room, she returned for the newly-painted canvas and a draping cloth. With the fabric tucked beneath her arm, she carefully carried the portrait to the easel, thankful that Baxter was safely locked away in the bathroom.

Taking a step back, she admired the painting one more time before pulling the drape over it, hiding her work from the world. For now. Her heart swelled with pride. This was her finest piece ever, of that she had no doubt. But then, she *had* painted this one with so much love.

Madison had just stepped out of the shower and plopped onto the chair in front of her dresser when Charity and Brody pounded up the stairs.

"We're home," Brody shouted.

"Hi, Mom, gotta rush to get ready," Charity's voice filtered through to the master bedroom.

Brody strode into the room, hands in his jeans pockets. "You're not ready yet?" He glanced at the Tag Heuer on his wrist.

Towel wrapped tightly around her body, Madison lifted her brush and pulled it through her wet hair with a sigh. "It was quite a morning getting everything organized, but it all looks amazing. Fit for a princess." She twisted around to look at Brody. "You did come in through the kitchen door, right?"

Nodding, Brody chuckled. "Avoided the party area, as you instructed...several times."

"Good." Madison turned back to attend to her hair, her gaze constantly flitting to Brody's reflection in the mirror.

"I'll just change out of these jeans and T-shirt into something a little more—" Brody bowed and his hair fell across his face. Rising, he raked the long fringe back. "Regal. Then I'll take a stroll downstairs to admire your handiwork."

Madison set the brush down and moaned, the heavy sigh more exaggerated than the last. The need to unburden her hectic morning to her husband overwhelmed. He'd spent the past few hours relaxing with their daughter; he had no idea how stressful her morning had been. And he *should* know.

"What a morning...cooking, baking, cleaning, setting up..."

"I told you to get caterers in."

Madison narrowed her gaze. "And I told you I could do it way better. Besides, I did get help with the cake and having prepared much beforehand, it was mostly a matter of popping things into the oven and then plating them. I'd barely finished the last batch of sausage swirls when the bakery arrived with the cake. It looks amazing. But between them and me fighting for working space in the dining room, and Baxter under our feet, I eventually had to lock the poor pooch in our bathroom. To compound matters, before I could take a shower, I had to first clean up all the pee and poop, not to mention the toilet roll he'd managed to unroll and drag merrily across the entire bathroom. Yes, through all his smelly business."

"You poor baby." Brody wrapped his fingers around her bare shoulders. Leaning forward, he kissed her cheek.

Madison continued, "In fact, the pup's still in there. So as soon as you or Charity are ready, one of you will need to take him outside. But please, make sure he doesn't get loose in the house as he could wreak havoc."

Brody straightened. "I'm sorry you had such a rough morning. I would've been here to help, but you insisted that Charity needed to be out of the house all morning. And although I love to cook, I couldn't have handled that menu on my own. Tell you what. I'll make it up to you with a romantic dinner after work one night during the week. Okay? Charity can sleep over at Sandy's house."

Thank heavens for Sandy, always willing to have Charity sleep over when Madison and Brody needed time alone, usually to make up after a tiff. And of course, Charity was always eager to spend time with Melinda, not only her best friend but Sandy's daughter too.

Madison took her hat off to her friend, raising a daughter on her own. It couldn't be easy. Fortunately, Sandy's late husband had left her well provided for after he passed away six years ago, so at least she didn't have to work two jobs as some single mothers do. And in all that time, Sandy had never so much as looked at another man. Grant had been her life, her soulmate.

As Brody was hers.

Madison watched in the mirror as Brody whipped off his T-shirt and grabbed a fresh dress shirt from his closet. A pale blue that complemented the color of his eyes. His back muscles sculpted like a Michelangelo statue as he lifted his well-toned arms and shrugged into the fancier threads. Eight years her senior, Brody was still as good looking at forty-three as the day she'd met him. She never tired of admiring him.

Okay, enough gawking. You have guests arriving in less than thirty minutes.

"So what did you and Charity get up to this morning?" she asked as she turned the can of hair mousse upside down and pressed the trigger. A ball of white foam formed in her palm. She quickly fingered it into her hair as Brody flashed a smile.

"What didn't we get up to? First I took her for breakfast at Crepes—"

"Great choice. She loves that place. Did she have her usual—?"

"Strawberry banana pancakes," they said in unison, laughing.

"After which, we test drove a couple of small, second hand cars." He winked as he stepped into a pair of dark blue trousers then pulled them up around his waist. "You know, befuddle her a bit, just in case she has any inkling that we've already bought her a car."

Brody slid his feet into a pair of tan leather shoes with monk straps, then snagged Madison's brush from the dresser. He brushed his hair back, tying it once again in the signature short ponytail that hung just over his collar.

So artsy.

So Brody Peterson.

Returning her brush to the dresser, Brody said, "There, I'm done. I'll take the dog out—on a leash—before having a gander at all your hard work."

"Thank you, honeybunch." Madison blew him a kiss then lifted the hairdryer. She paused before flicking on the switch. "Baxter will need to be returned to the bathroom before everyone arrives. Can you just imagine him being let loose at the party? My mother, for one, would have a notable fit."

"Your wish is my command, my darling." Another gallant bow from her knight in shining armor.

By the time Brody returned with the leash, Madison was halfway through drying her hair. It was the wild look for her today. A little hair gel added to the mousse, a little scrunching here and there, and she'd be done. Then she could put on her makeup and get dressed. She watched Brody's reflection as he slipped into the bathroom for a few minutes before Baxter dragged him out and down the passage.

Her mouth quirked. Good thing for that leash.

Madison finished styling her hair then quickly applied some light makeup. After years of practice, she had it down to ten minutes.

Excited, she stepped into the stunning new dress she'd bought for the occasion. A hugging lace sheath design in a pink so soft it was almost white. She loved the off-shoulder neckline that could be worn with the shoulders exposed or covered. The day was warm, so she opted to show a little skin. At least the above-elbow sleeves would make up some coverage. The dress was perhaps an inch or two shorter than she would've liked, but she did have the legs to pull it off. Besides, she was only thirty-five, not a hundred-and-thirty-five. It's not as if she was going out there as mutton dressed as lamb.

And Brody did enjoy having a beautiful wife at his side. As long as no other man gave her an ounce of attention. That always resulted in her husband's uncalled-for jealousy rearing its ugly head which led to huge arguments between them. Why, after all these years of marriage, did he still seem so afraid of losing her? And if she asked him the reason for his insecurities, it merely led to more fighting.

Madison had even plucked up the courage to ask Faith about it once. Brody's sister said she had no idea, but pointed out that Brody had always been like that, even with her and their brother, Tyler.

It was as if Brody was terrified to lose anyone close to him.

Madison sprayed a little of her favorite perfume on her pulse points, enjoying the soft, floral notes. She took one more look at herself in the mirror. Perfect. Now it was time to get downstairs. Her guests would be arriving soon, and Brody and she had even more wonderful surprises planned for Charity besides the car and the painting.

As she turned to go, Brody entered the bedroom.

He stopped dead, jaw slapping the floor. His eyes widened. "You're not wearing *that* are you? To our daughter's birthday party? Who's the sixteen year old here?" he snapped. "You, or Charity?"

His words stung. Disbelief washed over Madison, and she stared at him, mouth open, formulating a response.

She narrowed her eyes. "*This* is by no means a sixteen-year-old's dress. It's elegant and chic. I'd never allow Charity to wear something like this at her age."

Brody marched closer. He grabbed the hem. "It's far too short." Then he gripped the waist, tugging the fabric sideways. "And it's too tight."

Madison clamped her fingers over his, digging them into

21

Brody's skin. "Take your hands off me."

When Brody's hand fell away, Madison whipped the dress over her head, not caring that she'd probably messed her hair. Good thing she had opted for the wild look.

And wild was exactly how she felt right now, ready to kill.

She flung the dress across the bed then whipped open her closet, grabbing the first thing she laid her hands on—a formal pants set in taupe with matching shoestring beaded top and a long-sleeved chiffon jacket of the same color. It would do.

"There. Now I look more like the mother of the bride than the mother of the sweet-sixteen birthday girl," Madison snapped, shooting Brody a scathing look. "Satisfied?"

Why did he have such mood swings—one moment loving, irrational the next? Yes, she could just as easily flip the switch from hot to cold, but normally only when Brody pushed her buttons. Which he often did. And poor Charity bore the brunt of watching or hearing her parents' tiffs.

They needed to get their act together, for their daughter's sake.

Despite knowing that, it wasn't easy to change who they were.

Madison stiffened as Brody wrapped her in an embrace and whispered, "Much better, babe. Much better."

Lips pursed, Brody challenged Madison's glare.

She whirled around and flung her blond hair over her shoulder, uttering a suppressed scream before stomping out of the room in her high-heels. Good thing he hadn't suggested she change those shoes as well. Which might not have been a bad idea. For sure her feet would tire in those heels, and even wearing a pants suit, her legs still looked long and attractive.

And why was she so mad at him? The dress, although beautiful, was inappropriate for this affair. Sometimes she could be so feisty, he wondered if she wasn't an undercover redhead.

But he had to do what he had to do—his marriage needed protection. Not to mention their business. He wouldn't allow anything to threaten that. If his father had been more firm, maybe…

He pushed away the negative thoughts that pressed in. Today was not the day to revisit the moment that had forever defined him, changing the way he interacted with those close to him.

He would not be abandoned again. Not by anyone or anything.

As Madison marched down the staircase, Brody popped his head back inside Charity's room. He had left Baxter there moments before so the two could spend a little time together seeing as Charity had been out all morning, and she'd be separated from her precious pup once again this afternoon.

Spread out on her bed, Charity played with Baxter.

"Are you ready?" Brody enquired from the doorway. "Your mother's already downstairs. We should probably get down there too, but not before putting that little pooch back in our bathroom."

Propping her head on her elbow, Charity rolled onto her side and glanced at Brody. Her bottom lip jutted out. "Aw, Dad, do we have to? Poor thing has been locked up all day. Can't he join the fun?"

"No, Charity. Baxter will be too disruptive, and with so many people around, he could get overwhelmed and afraid. Not to mention the risk of someone tripping over him. He could get badly hurt." He didn't need to contend with a lawsuit. "It's best he's in our bathroom, out of the way. Just for today. Bring his bed and some toys. They'll keep him amused. You might even find he'll sleep the afternoon away. Your mom said he'd had a busy morning, so he's probably tired himself out. He's still only a small baby, remember."

Charity rolled her eyes. "You mean puppy, Dad. Dogs can't be babies; they're not humans." She slid off the bed, her white pumps landing on the plush pile. She pushed to her feet. The peachy fabric of her sleeveless dress swished around her body before the hemline settled around her knees. Madison had made a great choice, even though he knew it hadn't been easy getting their daughter to agree not to don her favorite denim cut-offs and red and white check shirt, and to wear this dress instead. For the sake of her visiting grandparents.

Pity Madison had lacked judgement in her own selection of clothing.

"I like your dress, Charity. Well-chosen."

Charity twirled around, and the skirt flared. Her mouth skewed to one side. "I feel like a bell."

Baxter lifted his head, ears pricking. With a sharp yap, he bounded off the bed to run circles around Charity as he nipped at her dress.

Brody grabbed him before the pup's teeth found their target and Charity was left having to change outfits as well. His fingers sank into Baxter's soft fur. "Well, you do know that bells have the sweetest sound."

After they'd settled the puppy in the bathroom, Brody linked his arm in his daughter's.

When they got to the stairs, she paused and turned to him. Uncertain eyes searched his. She sucked in a breath. "C–can I ask you something?"

"Sure, pumpkin. Anything." Brody had an inkling he knew what was on her mind.

"Did you and Mom just have a fight?"

Brody stroked a hand over her reddish-blond hair. "It was nothing, princess. Just a minor difference of opinion, that's all. We're fine now." He hoped. Madison was pretty mad when she marched out of their bedroom.

Worrying her bottom lip, Charity offered him a brittle smile. "Okay... Because I really don't want anything to spoil my birthday. I'll never get this sweet-sixteen over again."

"Honey, nothing will mar your day. It's going to be the best day of your life, I promise."

With the sound of arriving guests filtering up from below, Brody proudly walked his daughter down the stairs. Despite their personal issues, he and Madison had managed to raise one amazing kid.

He glanced at Charity out the corner of his eye.

Kid? She was no longer a kid. When they hadn't been looking, she had blossomed into a beautiful young lady.

CHAPTER THREE

"CHARITY HONEY, come and see who the wind blew in," Madison shouted from the hallway. Excitement flooded over her earlier frustration at Brody and washed it away.

"Hey, birthday girl," Faith, Brody's sister and Charity's favorite aunt called.

Charity shrieked, running into the hallway where the first arrivals stood. "Aunt Faith!" She wrapped her arms around Faith in an affectionate hug.

When Faith released her niece, she leaned back to take a good look at her. "You look so beautiful."

A blush washed Charity's cheeks. "Like my *dress*? Not too often you see me in one of these." With a roll of the eyes and a laugh, she twirled around.

Faith smoothed a hand down the soft chiffon of Charity's skirt. "It's gorgeous. Did your mom choose it? She has such amazing taste. This X-line is perfect for your petite figure, and I absolutely adore the lace bodice."

Madison stepped forward, not quite willing to take all the credit, even though she could. "We both decided on this one, although it took some convincing to get Charity to dress this fancy for her party."

"Backed against a brick wall, this *was* my best option." Charity shrugged, a smile cracking the thin line of her pursed lips.

"Well, it's beautiful and a most fitting choice." Faith handed Charity a small gift bag. "Just a little something special from me to you. We'll put your birthday gift on the gift table."

Charity peeked inside. "A new prayer journal! Oh, thank you, thank you, thank you." She withdrew the journal, covered in bright red poppies, and hugged it to her chest, the gift bag dangling from her fingers. "In the nick of time. My last one is almost full."

She dropped the book inside the gift bag then set it down on the console table behind her. As Charity turned back, she froze, staring at the guests who'd just stepped through the front door. She fist pumped the air. "Michael! Yes!"

Madison's heart warmed at the joy on her daughter's face. Charity loved her cousin, one year her junior. When the two were together, they weren't only joined at the hip, they were stuck together like conjoined twins.

Hugging, the two cousins bounced up and down as they talked over each other.

Next, Charity wrapped her arms around her Uncle Charles as he tried to squeeze past her and Michael. Madison had to admit that there was a time she hadn't liked Charles much—he'd seemed so detached from everyone. But Faith's accident nearly two years ago had definitely changed him.

Although Faith always said that God had done the transforming work.

"Wh–what are you all doing here? I didn't know you were coming to the party." Charity's face beamed. "It's a pretty long drive from Colorado to Kansas."

"We didn't drive," Charles said. "We would've had to leave at five this morning to make it here on time. Due to my work commitments on Monday morning, and Michael leaving the same day on a missions trip with our church to Africa, we opted to fly because Michael and Faith wouldn't hear anything about missing this birthday. I'm glad to be here too."

"Africa?" Charity squealed. She grabbed Michael's hands and the two jumped up and down. "You're going to Africa? That's so awesome. I wish I could go too."

Over my dead body.

Madison brushed a hand over Charity's head and smiled. "Maybe next time, honey."

Outside, a car pulled to a stop, drawing everyone's attention to the open portal. Three doors slammed shut, and then a baby cried.

Charity's jaw dropped. "No. Way."

"Yes way." A warm smile spread across Brody's handsome face.

Madison's anger melted. She never could stay angry with him for long.

Brody stepped across to Faith as Charity and Michael dashed outside, shouting, "Uncle Tyler! Aunt Hope! Leia!" Tyler, Hope, and their nine-month-old had also flown in for this special occasion from Florida.

Brody drew Faith into his arms. "Hey sis. It's good to see you. Thanks for coming." He glanced down at her leg. "How are you doing?"

Faith flashed one of her familiar bright smiles, the ones where her inner peace shone through. Faith's glass was always half full. Madison envied that in her.

"I'm well," Faith said. "We're all well. Life in Loveland is good."

"And your leg?" Madison touched Faith's arm lightly.

Faith shrugged. "Still a slight limp. Maybe it's something I'll have to resign myself to living with. And why not? The apostle

Paul was given a thorn in the flesh to keep him from being conceited; maybe this is mine. I can definitely attest to the fact that God's grace has been more than sufficient for me. It's amazing—sometimes you don't realize just how strong God is, until you are weak."

Brody motioned toward the door. "Should we go meet our new niece? Not that she's exactly brand new."

So typical. Brody always got the jitters when Faith began talking about spiritual things. Then again, Madison hadn't always encouraged Faith to share her beliefs either. Perhaps she should change that. Maybe God would be able to help her figure out Brody's underlying problem, why he sometimes acted the way he did.

Standing near the draped portrait, the white noise of chatter drowning out the soft music from the stereo, Madison sipped her drink and surveyed the guests. Some sat on the couches, some on the dining room chairs that had been moved against the wall, while others stood around the dining room table, snacking on the treats she had spent days preparing.

Shortly after Charity had opened her gifts, the five typical teens spilled outside onto the porch, eager to be away from the adults. Thankfully, the wind had died down somewhat, because Madison didn't relish the idea of Charity's dress doing a Marilyn Monroe on steroids.

Everyone appeared to be having a good time, especially Chad, the unexpected plus one on the arm of Jeanette, her very sassy, very single friend who, at the time of the invitation, had vowed she was done with men and would be attending on her own. But then, Madison could understand why Chad had swept Jeanette off her feet. Dashing good looks and a body to match—not to mention his flirtatious charm—could do that to a girl. Especially a girl like Jeanette. Though she'd tried, the woman really couldn't live without a man.

Madison's mother came to stand beside her, cup and saucer in hand. Madison had pulled out her finest tableware for her mother's visit. She gently touched her lips to the rim of the fine bone china teacup. Pinky in the air, she took a sip.

Setting the cup down carefully on the saucer, her mother said, "Once again, Madison darling, I'm so sorry we were late."

Madison waved her hand, dismissing her mother's repeated apology. "Only thirty minutes, Mother. There's no need to keep apologizing. Frankly, I think your timing was perfect. Everyone had arrived and settled, and you didn't need to contend with the craziness that goes along with guests arriving one after the other."

Hopefully that consolation would finally settle her mother's mind. If there was one thing James and Virginia Harding-Forbes disliked, it was *not* being on time.

"Besides, there was nothing you could do about the delay in taking off from LaGuardia, or the added setback collecting your rental at Emporia Municipal Airport." Madison would have loved to add that perhaps the universe was telling them not to come, but that wouldn't be prudent.

She pasted a smile on her face. "At least the asphalt runway was long enough for Daddy's company jet to land. A far better way to travel to Kansas than the six-hour commercial flight to Wichita, plus an eighty-minute road trip to Cottonwood Falls."

"Tell me about it. Oh, I well remember those journeys before your father made CEO, able to enjoy the perks that go with such a responsible position. But why you and Brody must live so off the grid, Madison, is beyond me. You should move your business to New York. We have a lot of connections. You'd be set up in no time."

"Mother! Cottonwood Falls is hardly off the grid. Besides, we love raising Charity out here in the country. There's an innocence we can offer her here that we can't in a big city. And I'll have you know that our business is doing just fine."

Then why are you entering Art USA, wanting to put Peterson Galleries on the map?

Madison dismissed the thought.

Her mother's mouth thinned into a tight line. She lifted the cup again and sipped daintily.

"At least having the jet at Daddy's disposal makes life so much easier for you. Especially seeing as you need to return tonight for his important breakfast tomorrow morning."

"Yes. We will be heading back long before the sun sets. I do wish we could've stayed longer, but it just wasn't possible. We barely managed to squeeze this day trip in."

Thank the good Lord they couldn't linger. Although she loved her mother and father, an afternoon in their presence—especially her mother's—was usually more than enough. Besides, the house was full with Brody's siblings—her parents would've had to overnight in Emporia if they'd wanted to stay longer.

"Well, I'm going to find your father. He has to try those sausage swirls before there are no more left. Did you get them from a bakery in Emporia? I'll have to try and pick some up on the way back to the airport."

"I baked them."

Mother's brows quirked. "Really? I am impressed, Madison. Well then, perhaps when you come to visit us in New York, you could bake a batch or two."

"That wouldn't be wise, Mother. Think of all those calories. Rather keep temptation far away than risk your beautiful figure."

With a slight shrug and a pout, Mother turned to go. "You're probably right."

Madison twisted around and stared out of the window to the porch outside. Huddled around a table, the teens laughed and joked and chatted, each vying to be the loudest. Yes, she could hear them from where she stood inside. It was good to see that Michael had soon renewed his acquaintance with Melinda and made friends with Ethan and Shana. All three teens were in Charity's class, although Ethan was a year older than the girls because he'd flunked the ninth grade. It wasn't that he was dumb; the boy was just far more interested in figures than he was in numbers. She'd need to keep a close eye on him around her daughter.

Further away on the lawn, two younger children chased each other around, their non-stop energy exhausting to watch. Charity had never really been one of those hyper kids, preferring to be rooted in one spot when outdoors, painting with her parents. But in recent years, Charity's interest in the activity had waned, and Madison often wondered whether their daughter would ever follow in her and Brody's footsteps. Instead of a brush and palette, Charity preferred to spend her time behind the pages of a book, or with her Bible, journal, and pen. That's if she wasn't hanging out with Melinda and Shana.

Madison turned away from the window to see Brody heading toward her. Coming to a stop beside Madison, he slid his arm around her waist and gave her a light squeeze. "Are you ready?"

She drew in a breath and nodded. The painting was the last gift for Charity to receive. Well, almost the last. The final one was parked at Clifford's place on the other side of town.

Rapping his knuckles against the window, Brody drew the teens' attention. He beckoned for them to come inside. Once they'd filed through the entrance to the living room, Brody tapped Madison's glass with a teaspoon, one he must've snagged earlier from the dining room table.

The buzz in the house quieted and heads turned their way.

Brody flashed a charming smile. "Friends and family, thank you for sharing this special day with Madison and me. Some of you have come from far—my sister, Faith, and her family from my home state, Colorado; my brother, Tyler, and his lovely wife and baby from sunny Florida; and James and Virginia—Madison's parents—all the way from the Big Apple. As for the rest of you…" his soft chuckle floated on the air, "well most of you know each other." Was he kidding? Everyone knew everyone in Cottonwood Falls. Brody must've been referring to Chad. He hailed from Emporia according to her friend.

Pointing to the easel, Brody said, "I know you've all been wondering what's hiding beneath this cloth—as has the birthday girl—and you've all been good not to peek."

Brody offered Madison a proud smile. "My beautiful wife has one more special gift for Charity, one our daughter has known about but never seen." Brody motioned with his hand for Charity to join them. "Come closer, honey."

Charity made her way across the oak laminate flooring, her heels clicking with each step, a blush coloring her cheeks.

"Now you all know just how talented my wife is," Brody continued, unashamedly blowing Madison's trumpet, "but *this* piece of work will bowl you all over. Guaranteed."

He leaned in closer to Madison and whispered, "Will you do the honors."

Eager for Charity to see her portrait, Madison reached up and carefully removed the drape.

Gasps sounded from around the room, the loudest from Charity. And not because she was standing the closest to Madison.

Both hands covered her mouth before she flung her arms around Madison's neck. "Oh, Mom, I love it! I can barely wait until I'm old enough to hang that in my own place. My first Peterson masterpiece."

"Well, I think until such time, your grandmother and I should look after that for you." Madison's father's voice boomed from where he and her mother sat in a nearby couch. "It's a fine piece of art and we'd be honored to have it hanging with our collection of rare works."

Laughing, Charity wagged a finger at her grandfather. "Oh no, Grandpa, no you don't. You're not getting your hands on this piece. I'll never get it back if you do."

Madison's arm slid around Charity's shoulder and she gave her daughter a light hug. "Don't worry, honey, we'll hang it safely in our home until you have a place of your own one day." She brushed a light kiss to Charity's silky tresses. "Just don't grow up *too* fast, sweetheart."

Wiggling out of her mother's embrace, Charity raised her shoulders in a cheeky shrug aimed at her grandparents. "You'll just have to get Mom to paint another one for you."

Madison shook her head. "No, no, no... *This* painting is one of a kind." And she intended to keep it that way. Her parents couldn't always have everything their hearts desired.

One by one, the guests came up to admire Madison's artwork and ask her questions. Sandy was the last. At least Madison hoped so. Arms folded, legs slightly spread, the two friends stood in front of the canvas staring at the life-like rendition of Charity.

"You've outdone yourself, Madison. Really outdone yourself."

"Thanks." Madison flashed Sandy a smile then returned her attention to the painting. Should she have made the sky bluer, the wheat a lighter gold?

"Do you want to know what I think?" Sandy's voice came once again from beside her.

Still focused on the flaws she thought she saw, her own worst critic, Madison replied, "What do you think, Sands?"

"That *this* is the one." Sandy touched Madison's arm.

Madison turned to look into her friend's brown eyes, alive with excitement. "W–what are you saying?" As if she didn't know.

"My friend, this is your best work ever." Lowering her voice, Sandy whispered, "You *have* to enter this painting into the Art USA contest you told me about. This is a winner. This is Kansas on a canvas."

A smile tugged at the corner of Madison's mouth. "Funny, that's exactly what Brody said."

"Well, your husband has a keen eye for art. Have you told him about the contest yet?"

Madison shook her head. "I'm worried it'll set him off on some tirade." She sighed. "Maybe I should just enter and *if* I make it to the second round, worry about telling him then."

"Girl, do whatever you have to. Just don't let this opportunity go by. I have a feeling you'll always regret it if you do."

Sandy was right. Madison would always wonder if she could have won with this painting. And surely Charity wouldn't object to her entering it?

Linking her arm in Sandy's, she leaned her head closer and whispered, "You're right. As always."

A smug smile curved Sandy's mouth. "I know."

Madison pursed her lips then huffed, her mind made up. "Okay, I'll do it. I'll submit my entry this week. But I'm not telling Brody, or Charity, until I absolutely have to." And if her husband didn't like the idea, he could lump it.

CHAPTER FOUR

PRIDE SWELLED Brody's chest as he watched from the other side of the living room. One by one, friends and family oohed and aahed over Madison's painting. His wife was so talented, and there was no doubt in his mind that if he exhibited the painting of Charity in their gallery, it would sell instantly. Plus, it would likely fetch one of the highest prices ever for a Peterson canvas. Already his father-in-law had offered him a ridiculous sum, suggesting Madison paint another for Charity, seeing as his granddaughter wouldn't have her own place for a few years. Brody had restrained himself from telling Madison's father exactly where to go. Through gritted teeth, he'd declined as gracefully as was possible so as not to cause a scene.

Without warning, apprehension dug its sharp talons into Brody's heart, pride quickly making way for his insecurities. As so often happened.

What if Madison became like—

No! He didn't want to return to the phobias and fears that had plagued him since he was ten. He couldn't allow his issues to sour Charity's birthday. And they easily could if he allowed himself to slip into a dark mood.

Needing something to take off the edge, Brody made his way through the house to the study. He shut the door then hurried over to the liquor cabinet where he poured himself a strong drink. In one fluid movement, he swigged back the amber liquid. His throat warmed, then his stomach, and his eyes slowly closed. Palms to the console table, he lowered his head and took several deep breaths.

In. Out.

In. Out.

He poured a second drink and sipped this one slowly.

Once calm had washed over him, Brody returned to the party. Hopefully no one would notice the alcohol on his breath. Still, he should do something to mask the fact that he'd had a drink. Well, two drinks. He'd seen some breath mints on the dining room table. Or were they on the coffee table in the living room?

Brody's gaze darted around the room as he searched for those mints. And his wife. Best he avoided her until he found something to mask the Scotch.

Unsuccessful at finding the breath fresheners amongst the array of half-eaten platters, Brody headed outside. Perhaps the best place for him to hide for a while.

A strong wind hit his face as he stepped onto the empty porch. Well, that would certainly explain all of their guests being inside— even the teens. In the distance, the sky had darkened. Gray mammatus clouds puffed overhead like gigantic cottonwood balls, harbingers of an impending storm. Hopefully it wouldn't develop into something worse, like a tornado.

Madison burst through the door, a large knife in her hand. "I've been looking all over for you. Charity needs to cut her birthday cake as my parents need to leave soon—they're concerned about those clouds." She tipped her chin to the heavens. "As is their pilot."

"I think they're right to be concerned. I hope it stays out there though and misses us." Maybe he should have a word with his brother and sister, ask them to pray.

"I thought it better to fast track our planned events for today, so Clifford and Amanda have just left to get the car from their house. They'll be back fairly soon. Hopefully there'll be enough time for Charity to cut that cake before they return." Madison slid her arm in Brody's and leaned into his shoulder. "So, where were you?"

"The bathroom," he lied, pressing his lips to Madison's head. He allowed the kiss to linger.

Madison turned to look up at him, her brows slowly narrowing as she eased back to stare him in the eye. "Have you been drinking? Today of all days?"

"Only two small tots," he defended himself. "You know what crowds do to me." *And your father.*

Madison released her hold on him, one hand moving straight to her hip. "Twenty people, *all* family and friends, isn't exactly a crowd. Really, Brody, you've been acting weird all day. Pull it together, for our daughter's sake. If you do anything to mess up this day, I swear—" She marched to the door and yanked it open.

"I won't," Brody said toward her back as he followed her inside.

In the dining room, Brody took his place next to the cake table, Madison beside him. Having no glass in hand or spoon to tap against it this time, Brody drew in a deep breath. He pasted on his most charming grin. Then, raising his voice, he said, "Folks, Charity's going to cut her birthday cake now."

The buzz of chatter died down.

Brody continued. "I'm sure you've all been waiting for this moment, although I do think that cake looks way too good to eat."

Hear, hears rose around the room.

While Madison pressed the sixteen pink candles into the fondant beside the peonies, Brody's gaze settled on Charity.

"Honey, come closer—it's *your* cake; you need to cut it. I, for one, can't wait to sink my teeth into all that sweetness." Hopefully Charity would get a good view through the dining room's window as his gym buddy, Clifford, drove that bright yellow bug into their backyard.

Standing in front of the cake table, Charity's gaze oscillated between Brody and Madison. "Thanks, Mom and Dad, this has been the best day ever. Nothing can top this."

Hearing the distinctive sound of the Volkswagen Beetle, Brody pointed through the window. Perfect timing.

"Nothing? Not even that?" The small, yellow car pulled up on the grass outside, horn honking loudly, a big red bow adorning its curved hood. His friend's large frame filled the small car's interior. They probably should have chosen someone with less muscle to drive the car to their house.

Charity squealed in unabashed delight. Forgetting all about the cake, she squeezed through the guests, Brody and Madison following close behind. Unable to contain her excitement, she dashed out the back door toward the vehicle, holding tightly to the hem of that flowing dress. Tendrils of reddish-blond lifted in the wind. "I can't believe it! I can't believe it!" she cried, and if it weren't for that dress, Brody was certain she would've jumped and twirled too.

Clifford clambered out of the car.

Without waiting, Charity slid behind the wheel and honked the horn again. Never before had he seen *such* a wide smile on her face. Well, maybe when she was five and got her own paints, canvas, and easel, "Just like Mommy's and Daddy's," she'd said.

She looked up at Brody through the driver's window. "Oh, Dad, she's beautiful. Can we take her for a test drive? Pleeeze?"

How did he say no to that? Not that easily, but they had guests anxiously waiting for that cake he'd so eloquently sold them on.

And none more so than his in-laws, but for very different reasons. James Harding-Forbes had one eye on the car, and the other on those dark, gray clouds. Brody couldn't keep anyone waiting while he took a joyride with his daughter.

"In a while, Charity. I promise." Brody opened the car door. "First I think you need to light those birthday candles and cut your cake, hmm? Your grandparents are anxious to get ahead of that storm."

"I agree," Madison said from behind. "There'll be plenty of time soon enough to enjoy this birthday gift."

Reluctantly, Charity stepped out of the car. Happy tears brimming, she flung her arms around Brody and Madison's necks then quickly let go to grab her whipping skirt. "Thank you, Mom and Dad. Thank you so much."

She gave Brody a light smack on the shoulder. "And you... Test driving all those second-hand cars this morning. I really thought I was getting one of those...maybe. I definitely did *not* expect this." With a sniff, she dabbed the corners of her baby-blues.

"Well, you can thank your grandparents for that." Brody tipped his head to where his father-in-law stood nearby. Then he leaned in to Charity and whispered, "They were the ones who insisted we buy this particular car for you—footed half the bill to ensure it happened."

Charity hurried over to her grandfather and wrapped one arm around his neck, the other still holding tightly to that dress. "Thank you, Grandpa." She looked around. "Where's Grandmother?"

"Still safely inside." James chuckled. "Didn't want to get her hair messed up. Not sure how she thinks she's going to get to the car when we leave."

Likely she'd have James drive that rental as close to their back porch as he could so as to make a quick dash to the car.

"Then I'll thank her once we're back inside." She linked her arm into her grandfather's and started toward the house. "C'mon. We have a cake to cut."

Soon Charity had sliced the entire bottom tier, and neat triangular wedges were handed out to the guests. All the teens and kids went back for a second helping.

After James and Virginia bade a hasty farewell—their pilot calling to say they had to leave within the next forty-five minutes or they could risk being unable to take off—Brody settled into one of the dining room chairs that lined one wall. Seated beside Hope and Tyler—baby Leia fast asleep in her mother's arms—Brody cast his gaze around the room as he forked another piece of red velvet into his mouth. His eyes settled on Madison where she stood in front of Charity's portrait talking to Faith and Charles.

Brody glanced at his brother. "'Scuse me for a moment. I think it's time I encouraged my wife to sit down and relax."

"I agree," Hope said. "She's been on her feet all day."

Madison's back was toward Brody as he strode in her direction.

Just then, Faith gave Madison a hug before she and Charles walked away.

The place beside his wife was barely vacant before the good-looking guy who'd arrived on the arm of Madison's single friend, Jeanette, swooped into the empty spot. Chad, if he remembered correctly.

Standing beside Madison with his arms folded, legs spread-eagled, Chad stared at Madison's artwork. Brody had been in this business long enough to know a fake art enthusiast when he saw one. So if Chad wasn't really interested in art, what was the attraction for this dude?

Anger and insecurities boiled in Brody's gut like a witch's brew.

Madison.

Stopping close enough to eavesdrop, Brody joined his friends,

Duncan and Clifford, where they huddled near the living room entrance, enjoying yet another piece of cake. Not paying any attention to their conversation, Brody heard Chad say, "You really paint this?"

Brody turned just enough to see his wife and the interloper out the corner of his eye. Madison pointed to her signature in the bottom right-hand corner. "I guess so. That *is* my signature right there."

Chad leaned in to take a closer look then flashed Madison a cheesy grin. "Madison Peterson. That's a nice name...the first one."

Madison's soft laugh floated on the air. "Why, thank you."

Chad shifted on his feet, facing Madison more than the portrait he'd been so interested in just a moment ago. "Thanks for not kicking me out of your party. I know I wasn't exactly invited."

Madison touched his arm lightly. "My daughter's party. And of course you were invited. Well, maybe not formally, but you're here with Jeanette, and Jeanette had the option to bring a plus one."

Chad leaned in closer to Madison, and lowered his voice. Brody could barely make out his words as he said, "You know, I've been waiting all afternoon for the opportunity to speak to you alone. I just wanted to let you know how incredibly attractive and sexy I find you."

That was it. Brody had heard enough. He wasn't going to stand idly by, pretending to chat with his friends, while just a few feet away some stranger with more brawn than brain tried to make out with his wife.

Brody stomped over to where Madison and Chad stood. He brushed past his wife and dug his fingers into Chad's arm. "Right, buddy, I've heard enough. I believe you've overstayed your welcome. It's time for you to hit the road. Bye-bye." He waved his fingers at Chad.

"Brody! You're making a scene." Madison reached for Brody's hand on Chad's arm. "Chad and I were just talking."

Brody's jaw slackened, his eyes widening in disbelief. "Talking? Looked more like flirting to me." Brody failed to keep his annoyance in check. "Whatever, Madison, it's time for this guy to leave and for you to join me and my family.

Madison shifted between Brody and Chad. "No!" Her sapphire-blue eyes glinted, challenging Brody's authority.

"No?" He did not expect she'd favor some stranger over him.

"No! First you dictate what I should, or rather, shouldn't wear. And now you want to tell me who I can and can't talk to?" Madison's nostrils flared, and her eyes flashed with rage. "Why don't *you* leave, Brody? And while you're gone, maybe you can search for a better mood."

A smirk tugged at Chad's mouth, and all Brody wanted to do was wipe it from the man's face. With his fist.

Brody shoved at Chad.

Chad stumbled back a few steps.

Whirling around, Brody stomped across to where Charity stood talking to her cousin and friends. "Charity, come. Time for that test drive," he barked.

Dear Jesus,

One day… just one perfect day is all I wanted for my birthday. Mom and Dad couldn't even give me that. Oh, they almost did. But then they blew it. Big time. Their actions spoiled the rest of the day. I'm just glad that my grandparents had already left and weren't there to see it.

By the time Dad and I got back from his "test drive"—more like Nascar—the guests who hadn't yet left were about to do so.

I was so scared. Dad drove way faster than he should have, especially with the strong winds blowing outside. I thought for sure my little yellow car would flip right over. Then there was the alcohol smell on Dad's breath. Well, You know I haven't prayed so hard in my life. I've only just turned sixteen, and I've so much life left to live, so much I still want to do—for myself and for You.

Thank You for bringing my family to my birthday. It was good to have Michael here to talk to. And he was a great shoulder to cry on because his parents have been through some recent troubles too. And Aunt Faith...oh, she always knows how to make me feel better.

I'm glad Michael and I could sit in my room with Baxter and chat. My beautiful pup, and cousin, soon lifted my spirits. I really didn't want to be with my family tonight—the atmosphere was so thick around the dinner table you could cut it with a cake knife. Mom and Dad weren't talking to each other, and the rest of the family tried their best to make light conversation. I'm sure everyone turned in way earlier than they'd anticipated. What a damper on the day.

But tomorrow is a new day, a fresh beginning, so I'm going to get up early, put on a happy face, and make cinnamon rolls for everyone. There's nothing like the aroma of freshly baked cinnamon rolls and brewed coffee to put one in a good mood for the day. I do hope it helps...especially for me. Maybe You could make sure that the morning sermon helps too. Aunt Faith said she would take me to church. Everyone else said they wanted to go too, even Mom and Dad. But You already know all that. I think it's Mom and Dad's way of trying to make things up to me for spoiling my party. Well, whatever it takes to see them come to know You. Right?

Anyway, I'm leaving all of their issues in Your hands, because only You can paint a beautiful picture of their lives. Even though they think they're quite capable, they aren't.

With love
Charity
(Always a princess in Your eyes)

P.S. Can You help me to find it in my heart to forgive my parents? Again. It seems that the older I get, the harder it becomes. I need Your divine help.

CHAPTER FIVE

STILL IGNORING Brody, the fourth day in a row, Madison poured a cup of coffee. A side plate with a slice of buttered toast firmly in one hand, her coffee in the other, Madison joined her husband and daughter at the hushed breakfast table.

Scenting fresh food, Baxter hurried over to Madison's side of the table, his claws clicking on the ceramic floor tiles.

Madison set the cup and plate down on the table, then gave Baxter a pat and a rub. She smiled at her daughter. "Morning, Charity."

Charity mustered a smile in return. "Morning, Mom." She had been sullen and unhappy after her birthday party ended so abruptly.

And even though Charity had hidden her sadness on Sunday morning behind cinnamon rolls, freshly brewed coffee, and a church service, once her cousin and favorite aunt had left, she became cheerless once again.

Madison knew her daughter was hurt, and she didn't blame her one bit.

Brody offered Madison a good morning which she refused to acknowledge. Since Saturday, Madison had only spoken to Brody when necessary. Never before had they let *this* many sunsets go down on their anger. Usually they'd explode like Mount Vesuvius and then make up not long after, the eruption quickly forgotten.

Sometimes she wondered if she didn't deliberately pick fights with her husband just for the sweet make-up sex, because with Brody it was oh so worth it.

But he had messed up big this time. He'd been totally unreasonable on more than one occasion on Saturday. Then he'd driven irresponsibly, *after* taking two drinks, with their most precious possession in the car with him, taking absolutely no heed of the impending storm. Fortunately, the F0 tornado had skirted through the Tallgrass Prairies National Preserve, fizzling out somewhere between Council Grove and Admire. Still, if Brody didn't care about hurting himself, fine, but she would not stand idly by while he put their only child's life in danger.

Yes, he wasn't drunk—not by a long shot—however, if he'd been pulled over by the cops, he might've dodged a DUI, but he wouldn't have escaped being charged for speeding. At least according to Charity.

And speeding tickets aside, what if he'd caused an accident? What if that tornado had turned and sucked that little yellow car up its funnel? Her daughter wouldn't have been following the yellow brick road to the Emerald City like the Wizard of Oz's Dorothy Gale, she would've been standing beside the pearly gates. And as for Brody, he'd have been knocking on the gates of hell.

Madison shuddered, the thought of heaven and hell scaring her.

Charity had been shaken when they'd returned, Madison finding her in tears in the bathroom upstairs shortly afterwards. For that, Madison found it hard to offer an olive branch this time, despite Brody's attempts at sweet talk, his soft touches in the middle of the night. Not even the preacher's words on Sunday morning about not allowing the sun to go down on your anger had been able to convince her to reconcile, to forgive her husband and put the fiasco behind them.

In fact, she'd been so mad at Brody that as soon as he'd left for the gallery on Monday morning and Charity had hopped on her bicycle, off to Melinda, Baxter quite happy to go for a ride in the wire pet basket up front, Madison had taken photographs of Charity's birthday portrait and then entered it into the Art USA contest. In the nick of time too. She hadn't realized the deadline was *this* Friday. Within three weeks, she'd know if she had made it into the finals.

Madison didn't know why, but she had the strangest intuition that she would. Crazy thought because she didn't know the caliber of the other entries…entries from all across America. What she did know was that the judges were ruthless art experts. And rightly so. Ellie Sanders's reputation was on the line here. They had to make sure they chose the most talented artist in the USA.

She had a one in fifty chance of winning if she *did* get into the next round.

Girl in a Field, she'd aptly named the piece while completing the online application.

Without so much as a glance at Brody, Madison set her coffee cup down and informed him that she would be working from home today.

"Home? But it's Wednesday. It's Ava's day off. You always come into the gallery on Wednesdays to help. Charity's portrait is complete now, so there's no need to be at home," Brody whined.

Madison's spine straightened like a steel rod. Staring into her cup of dark brew, she eased her shoulders back, her voice as icy as the Hudson River in January. "I'm quite sure you can manage on your own. After all, you love being in charge over everything, running the show, don't you?"

Pursing her lips, she turned to glare at Brody. "Besides, I *have* to be here—Charity's appointment for her GDL is this afternoon, or had you forgotten? *Somebody* has to drive her to the driver licensing office in Emporia. Or maybe you'd prefer she breaks the law and drives herself. Like father, like daughter, hmm?"

Charity shoved to her feet, the chair toppling over and clattering against the floor. "Stop it! Just stop it! If I can forgive you both for ruining my birthday—and believe me, it hasn't been easy—can't you just get over yourselves and forgive each other? Kiss and make up like you always do?" She fled the kitchen in tears, Baxter bounding after her.

"You happy now?" Brody thumped his coffee cup down and shoved to his feet, his chair scraping against the tiled floor. He snatched his cell phone and car keys from the table then stomped away.

Soon Madison heard the front door slam shut and Brody's SUV roaring up the street.

Ugh, she was only making things worse by harboring her anger. She needed to find a way to get past this.

Seated outside the driver licensing office in Charity's petite yellow car, Madison waited for her daughter to burst through the doors, excitedly waving her new driving permit. She had shifted into the passenger seat so that Charity could drive home. Charity could clock up the first thirty minutes toward the fifty driving hours required to have the restrictions lifted on her license within six months.

She wished she could be a fly on the wall in that building, but Charity had insisted she could do this alone, that she didn't need her mother chaperoning her.

The procedure shouldn't take too long. Armed with her DE-99 completion slip from her driver's education, Charity wouldn't need to undertake the knowledge or driving tests. Hopefully all that was required would be to pay the license and photo fees, have her picture taken and *voila*, she could get her license.

But when Charity exited the license office, it wasn't in the way that Madison had expected. No running or jumping or waving her permit in the air. Instead she trudged out slowly, shoulders slumped, head and eyes downcast.

Madison's heart squeezed. Had something gone wrong?

Charity opened the driver's door and sank into the driver's seat. She flicked a small card into the console box.

"H–how did it go?" Madison asked. "Did you get it?"

"Yeah, I got it."

"May I?" Madison reached for the card Charity had so carelessly discarded.

Charity shrugged. "Knock yourself out."

Madison lifted the card and stared at Charity's restricted driver's license permit. Her little girl could drive a car! Felt like yesterday she was still on a bicycle with training wheels.

"Congrats, honey. And that's a beautiful photo of you. Usually these official photos come out awful, but that's not the case here. You're so photogenic."

"Can we go now, Mom?"

"Um, sure. Would you like to go for a celebratory milkshake? We could go to Crepes. Maybe I could ask your father to join us?"

"I just want to go home." Charity tried a crooked smile, not very successfully.

Madison nodded. "Of course. But first, can I just say something?" She waited eagerly for Charity to refuse her request.

She didn't.

Madison reached over and took Charity's hands in hers. "I'm so sorry. Both your dad and I messed up. I've been blaming him, reluctant to make up...but we're both at fault." Even if it was

Brody's fault more so than hers. She could've taken a deep breath and let his mess-ups go the next day, not reacted the way she had, making the situation worse. "I promise you I'll fix things between your dad and me. Tonight."

Madison bumped Charity's arm with her elbow. "So what do you say? A small milkshake?"

A smile slowly curved on Charity's face. She lifted her eyes to meet Madison's. "Oh, all right. Maybe just a small one. Strawberry. You and me celebrating at Crepes does sound wonderful, Mom."

"Fantastic." Madison pointed to the ignition. "Well, what are you waiting for? Start the car. Oh, and how would you feel about sleeping over at Melinda tonight?"

"Why, are you planning on not only fixing things with Dad but making up?" Charity shot her a cheeky grin and waggled her brows. "I know exactly why you ship me off to my best friend from time to time, usually with the oddest excuses."

A blush warmed Madison's cheeks. She burst out laughing. "Guilty as charged."

"Then I'd love to sleep over at Melinda tonight. But will you ask Aunt Sandy if Baxter can come too?"

"Of course." Sandy had better take Baxter. She didn't need their new pup messing with her plans for tonight.

Smiling, Charity started the engine then paused before putting the stick shift into reverse. She gazed at Madison, sadness glazing her eyes again. "Mom, do you think you and Dad will ever go too far one day with your arguments? Like get a divorce, making me choose who to stay with? Because I don't want to choose. I love you both so much."

"Oh, honey, no...." Madison worried her lip. At least, she hoped not. But even she didn't feel that reassured by her answer. What if they did go too far one day and one of them sued for a divorce? There was no denying their arguments had escalated over the years—more frequent, more intense. Despite that, she loved Brody with all her heart. He was her man—always had been, always would be—and she never, ever wanted to place Charity in a position where she'd have to make a choice. Somehow Madison knew that neither she nor Brody would emerge from that fight the winner.

CHAPTER SIX

ALL DAY long, Brody chided himself for flying off the handle that morning with Madison. His wife wasn't the only one to blame for Charity being upset. Madison had every right to be angry over what had happened on Saturday. If the roles had been reversed and she'd been the one to drive irresponsibly with their daughter, he would also be ignoring her. He was getting his just desserts, that's all.

He needed to make things right. With Madison and Charity.

But first, his wife.

After Brody locked the gallery for the night—a little earlier than usual—he pulled his cell phone out of his jacket pocket and called Sandy.

He was about to give up hope that she'd answer when her voice suddenly sounded in his ear. "Brody. What can I do for you?"

"Hey, Sands, how are you?" Brody's voice dripped so sweet it made even him ill.

"I'm fine. What do you want?" Her clipped responses told Brody that he was in the dog box with his wife's best friend too. But what had he expected?

"Listen, I'm really sorry about my behavior on Saturday—

there's no excuse. And if it adversely affected you in any way, I'm sorry. Truly I am."

"Nope. Not me. My friend on the other hand…"

"And that's exactly why I'm calling." Brody stepped into a flower shop a few stores down from the gallery. Smiling at the florist, he pointed to the red, long-stemmed roses. Then, using hand gestures, he indicated his need for two dozen to be packaged in a long, elegant box. Guaranteed to melt Madison's heart. "I need to make things right with Madison. Do you think that Charity—?"

Sandy's heavy sigh cut him off. "Yes, she can sleep over tonight."

"Thank you, Sands. You're the best. Now just to come up with an excuse of why she needs to go to your place tonight."

"It's summer vacation. With no school, there's no need for excuses. But if it'll make you feel better, I'll get Melinda to invite her over for the night." There was a short pause before Sandy asked, "What time will you be home?"

"In an hour or so. I have a few things that need to be taken care of before leaving Emporia."

"Great. I'll call Madison, ask if Charity can sleep over, and then I'll drive to your place and pick her up long before you get there. Madison won't suspect a thing. Trust me."

Well that was easier than he'd thought it would be. "Thanks. I owe you one. Oh, another thing—can Baxter come too?"

"The dog can come, Brody."

Giving a fist pump, he hung up. *Yes!* He had the entire night to make things right with his wife. And he'd messed up so badly, it might just take all that time for her to forgive him and sweeten to his affections.

Brody paid for the flowers then exited the small, fragrant shop. Three more stops and he could head on home. Tonight, he planned to sweep his wife off her feet and win her favor once again.

"Ooh la la, don't you look amazing?" Sandy made Madison twirl around.

Madison chuckled nervously. "I hope I've made the right choice with this outfit. The first and last time I wore this dress likely started the mess Brody and I are in now. He didn't approve of it for Charity's party. I'm just hoping he might think differently for a more private and intimate affair."

Sandy's eyes widened. "Are you kidding me? What husband wouldn't want to come home to his wife looking like *that*?" Her eyes fluttered closed for a moment as she inhaled deeply. "Not to mention the delicious aromas wafting through the house and such a romantic table setting?" She pointed toward the dining room where Madison had set out her finest silverware, crystal, and china. An open bottle of their finest red wine aired on the table between the two place settings.

Sandy glanced at the packet of rose petals lying on the kitchen counter that Madison had picked up from the florist before she and Charity left Emporia. "I hope those are for the staircase, the bedroom, and your bed."

Heat rushed up Madison's neck to her cheeks. She buckled over, laughing.

"Bingo. I guessed right." Sandy wiggled her arms and hips in a triumphant jig. "You sure you don't want me to keep your daughter for two nights?"

The thought of two full nights and a day spread warm tingles though Madison's body. She fanned herself with her hand and chuckled. "Whew, is it hot in here or what?"

"No." Sandy offered her an innocent smile, and then winked. "If you two don't make up after all this, then I might as well drive you down to the Chase County Courthouse now."

For three days Madison had been certain Brody wanted things right between them, but after this morning, the way she'd goaded him…well, she wasn't so certain. That's why she'd pulled out all the stops for tonight. She was getting her marriage back on track.

Until the next time.

Whoa, where did that thought spring from?

"So, two nights?" Sandy waggled her brows and prodded Madison in the arm with her elbow before strolling over to the oven. She opened the dark glass door slightly, releasing a loud sigh as she savored the aroma of lamb roasting, hints of garlic and rosemary intermingling with the meaty scent. "Ooh, yum. Maybe we need to make that three nights. Oh, why not just let her stay until after the weekend?"

Thumbnail to her mouth to hide her smile, Madison's other hand clasped her waist. She raised her gaze to her friend. "That really won't be necessary. Tonight will be sufficient." Stepping forward, Madison turned off the oven. Dinner was ready. Hopefully Brody wouldn't be much longer.

A wide grin spread across Sandy's face as she twirled her blond hair into a knot on her head then let it go, sending a waterfall of gold cascading over her shoulders once again. "Oh, it might not be necessary, my friend, but it would be sooo nice, wouldn't it?"

Before Madison could answer, Charity and Melinda burst into the kitchen, an overnight bag in Charity's hand and Baxter safely tucked in Melinda's arms.

Charity leaned back against the refrigerator. "I'm ready, Aunt Sandy, although you do know I could've driven myself over. Have you forgotten that I have my own car now?"

"I know, sweetheart. But if you drove over, I would have missed out on seeing all that your mom has planned," Sandy said. "Besides, I'm sure neither you, nor your mom and dad want that gorgeous little car of yours getting damaged just yet by Baxter's sharp nails. At least in my older car, I don't mind."

"Yeah, I hadn't thought of that. I do want to keep my car looking as good as new for as long as possible. Can we go now, before my Dad gets home? We wouldn't want to get in the way of *anything*, would we?"

"Oh no, we wouldn't." Sandy pecked Madison on the cheek and whispered, "Get up to *everything* I wouldn't."

"Oh you…" Smiling, Madison prodded Sandy lightly in the chest. "*You* don't get up to anything. It's about time I found you a handsome widower."

Sandy pulled a face, shaking her head vigorously at Madison's suggestion. Was her friend really that adverse to the idea of falling in love again, or did she just pretend to feel that way because she was too scared to venture there?

From the front door, Madison waved goodbye. The moment they pulled away, she hurried back inside. Had to get those rose petals scattered.

The last pink petal drifted to the bed when Madison heard a sound behind her. She whirled around to see Brody standing at the bedroom door. Tucked under his arm was a long, elegant flower box—probably roses, red she hoped. In one hand he held a box of fancy chocolates. And was that her favorite perfume on the top of the chocolate box that his fingers barely managed to clamp around? Two paper pails of Chinese food hung from the fingers of his other hand.

Oh…

She had seen some sorry faces on Brody Peterson over the years, but today, even Winnie the Pooh's donkey friend, Eeyore, couldn't have pulled a more contrite face.

His smile uncertain, apologetic, Brody neared. "Did we have the same idea for tonight?"

Madison's gaze skittered around the room at the petals on the bed and the floor. Her mind backtracked to the trail leading all the way to the front door. Oh, her husband knew the moment he walked through that door what was on her mind.

"Maybe not the menu..." She swallowed hard, her mouth suddenly dry. "I do have wine with my meal."

His voice husky, Brody whispered, "You look incredible."

He set the flowers, chocolates, and perfume down on the tufted bench at the foot of their bed then twisted around for a moment to deposit the paper containers on her dresser. Gaze glowing with ardor, Brody pulled Madison into his arms. "Can you ever forgive me for being such a complete jerk? For being reckless and irresponsible."

Madison melted at his touch. Fighting did have its merits. "Can you forgive me too? I shouldn't have dragged this out as long as I did." She'd only hurt Charity in the process.

No need for long discussions, dissecting what they did or didn't do, what they said or didn't say, Brody's mouth claimed hers. All they needed in that moment was to feel the depth of forgiveness in each other's kiss.

The meals and wine forgotten, Brody and Madison satisfied the only hunger that mattered.

Lying beneath the cotton sheet in her husband's arms, summer twilight finally dimming the room, Madison trailed her fingers across Brody's stomach, tracing his well-defined six-pack. She buried her head in his chest and began to laugh softly.

Brody lifted his head from the pillow then tipped her face toward him. A lazy grin curved his lips, the five o'clock shadow coloring his jawline seeming darker in the low light. "And what is so funny?"

Madison shook her head. "I was just thinking how that dress doesn't seem to want to stay on my body for more than a few minutes."

Tightening his embrace, Brody pressed a kiss to her brow. "As much as I did love you in it, I much prefer you out of it."

A soft sigh escaped Madison's lips. Being here in bed with her husband in the afterglow of their love, all was right with their world once again. Simply picture-perfect.

"I'm so glad Sandy took Charity. It would be very difficult to make up like this with a teenager in the house." She chuckled once again, joy overwhelming her. She could just burst like a popped balloon.

Brody combed his fingers through her hair. "Me too. I was worried she might turn me down. She was pretty mad at me too. But I guess she knew we needed to kiss and make up, huh?"

Sheet tucked under her arms, Madison propped herself up on her elbow. Her hair spilled over her bare shoulder as she leaned her head on it. "Wait a minute... You spoke to Sandy?"

"Yes, just before I left the gallery. I needed to make arrangements with her for tonight."

Madison's laughter floated through the room again. "So did I. Earlier this afternoon. But she never said a word to me about your call when she fetched Charity."

Brody's low rumbles joined Madison's chuckles as they flopped back onto the pillows.

When their laughter subsided, Brody said, "Oh, she played us both, didn't she? But it shows how much she wanted us to work through our differences. She's a good friend, Madison."

"She is." Madison turned on her side and trailed her fingers through Brody's shoulder-length hair, his signature ponytail long gone. She pressed her lips to his and muttered, "But *you* are my best friend, even though we fight. Never forget it."

"I won't." Brody pecked her on the nose then shot upright in bed, his toned back on display for Madison to take in the muscles and contours. So perfect—like Michelangelo's David. He twisted around to her. "You hungry?"

Wearing only the sheet and a smile, Madison nodded eagerly. "Starved."

"Dinner in bed?"

Madison shoved at Brody's back. "Just get those paper pails, will you." She didn't mind the food being cold—she'd already feasted on something sizzling hot tonight.

CHAPTER SEVEN

AFTER WAVING goodbye to Brody, Madison shut the front door and headed to her studio. She had to finish the piece for the Stanleys today. Brody needed to ship the landscape off to Curt Stanley in California by next weekend, and it needed sufficient time to dry.

As she dabbed the canvas with the colors of a California sunset over the North Pacific Ocean—a little bit of vermilion covering the light blue background for the sun-kissed clouds, a touch of cobalt violet along the top right hand corner for the coming storm, and the light gray of buff titanium mixed with cadmium yellow on the left for the sunbeams streaking the sky—Madison mused on the past three weeks of paradise in the Peterson household since she and Brody had reconciled. She was happy. Brody was happy. But most of all, Charity was happy—especially because they'd attended church with her the past four Sundays. Madison had to admit the new minister was quite dynamic, even though most times his sermons made her shift uncomfortably in her seat. Of course, that first Sunday when they'd gone along with Faith and Tyler and the rest of the family, Madison had closed her heart to the words from the pulpit. But every week since then, she'd started to pay more attention to the sermons on God's love and grace and how God can forgive us, no matter what.

Brody, however, had grown restless of attending church every week. Madison knew the signs. With the family settled into a blissful period, he had made plans for them all to drive to Monument Rocks in Gove County on Saturday morning, a four and a half hour drive west and north, to do a little nightscape of the magnificent rocks and incredible skies. Already had permission from the owners to paint there at night. And the nearly full moon this weekend would give them perfect lighting on those seventy-foot chalk buttes and arches.

Charity had turned down her father's plans for a family weekend, opting to stay behind with Melinda and Sandy so that she could go to church on Sunday morning. She didn't want to miss the next installment of Pastor Andy's sermons on 'Who is God?'. "Besides, you know I'm not that into painting," she'd told Brody and Madison when Brody broke the news of the overnighter. "I'm just going to sit there and read, which I can do right here in Cottonwood Falls. Although I really love your work, Mom and Dad—truly I do—being outdoors with a palette and easel is your thing, not mine."

A shrill ringing snapped Madison out of her musing. She set her brush and palette down on the nearby counter overflowing with paints, brushes, and blank canvases. Shoving her hand in the back pocket of her jeans, she pulled out her phone.

"Sands, what's up?"

"Have you heard anything yet?" Angst laced her friend's voice.

Shoulders slumping, Madison released a heavy sigh. "Nothing yet."

"Argh, I can't stand this waiting."

Madison leaned her hip against the long counter that stretched the entire length of the wall. "Neither can I. Either way, we'll know by tomorrow. So it's not that much longer to wait."

Sandy wailed. "Tomorrow is twenty-four hours—give or take—too long, girl."

It was, but Madison didn't need to be reminded. For days now, she'd been counting the hours, heart pounding every time her phone rang, only to be disappointed once she'd answered.

"Sands, I–I have to go. I'm on a deadline to get this piece finished today. I'll call you the moment I hear anything. I promise."

"First one to hear…"

Madison smiled and pushed away from the counter. "First one to hear."

She hung up and shoved the phone back into her pocket. Then she picked up her palette and brush, her thoughts now focused on the Art USA contest and the imminent results. As she gazed at the impending storm she was busy painting on the canvas, Madison couldn't help but wonder if the past three weeks were the calm before *her* storm. If she was one of the fifty finalists, there was no doubt in her mind that there'd be a storm of note between her and Brody. But all she could do now was hunker down and weather it out *if* that happened.

After Madison had put the last brushstroke to the Stanley artwork, she added her signature to the bottom right-hand corner, signaling the completion of yet another Peterson masterpiece. A sense of accomplishment washed over her, but nothing like how she'd felt the day she finished Charity's piece.

And now that piece could change their lives.

Forever.

Then again, life could go on as usual, nobody besides her and Sandy being any the wiser that she'd tried and failed.

Strands of hair fallen loose from her ponytail tickled her face. She swiped them back behind her ears, her heart heavy…conflicted. She didn't want to risk her life with Brody—but she also didn't want him to forever block her path to ultimate success. Hopefully, if it came to it, he'd understand that she'd entered the contest for them—for Peterson Galleries. Getting the endorsement of Ellie Sanders… Well, that was huge.

Outside a dog yapped, just before the porch door banged shut.

"Hi, Mom, I'm home," Charity shouted as her footfalls pounded upstairs. Baxter's bark followed her. Still not willing to risk having Baxter damage her car with his claws, Charity had placed her pup in his wire pet basket, and cycled to Melinda's just before lunch.

Madison's phone rang, and she whipped the device out of her pocket. She frowned. Although she didn't recognize the number, she was very familiar with the 212 area code where her father had his Manhattan office. Her hands began to tremble, and she quickly sank into the bright green barrel chair nearby before her legs buckled beneath her.

"Madison Peterson," she answered, in the calmest voice she could muster.

"Miss Peterson!" a deep, male voice responded to her greeting.

"Mrs. Peterson," Madison corrected.

"I apologize, Mrs. Peterson, but maybe I could just call you Maddie?"

Her nerves quickly gave way to annoyance. Who *was* this person and why were they calling? And with such familiarity. Hopefully not another tactless telesales person.

Before she could respond, the man continued. "I'll take that as a yes." There was a brief pause as the man sucked in a breath. "Maddie, it's Robert Morris, but you can call me Rob. I'm the contest coordinator for Art USA." His New York accent rolled off his upper teeth with the distinctive and recognizable AW sound every time he uttered the word call.

Her heart thudded so hard against her chest, it hurt. *This* man could call her anything he liked, because if Art USA was contacting her *before* the notification deadline on Friday, it could only mean one thing.

"Maddie, congratulations on being our Kansas finalist with your entry, *Girl in a Field*."

Madison's hand flew to her mouth, her lungs constricting, refusing to give air. She gasped. "W–what? I–I can't believe it." Even though she'd been so positive about standing a good chance to make it to the finals, actually hearing those words spoken out loud came as a shock, albeit a pleasant one. "Really?"

"Yes, Maddie. And well deserved, I must add."

There was a moment's silence as Madison endeavored to process the news. Now she'd *have* to tell Charity. And Brody. Her daughter would be excited for her, she was certain. But her husband… Madison had a pretty good idea of how Brody would react, so telling him was something she did not relish. But it had to be done. She should probably do it over the weekend while they were stargazing at Monument Rocks. Or perhaps the following morning might be preferable. No point in ruining a romantic night in a magical place with her husband. Brody had said he had something special planned—she didn't want to risk spoiling his surprise.

"Maddie…?" Rob's voice pulled her back to the present.

"Oh yes, sorry, you were saying?"

"Please could you email me a high resolution headshot of yourself today? Your suggested travel itinerary will be sent to you within a day or two," Rob said. "Once you confirm your best travel times, we'll make the necessary hotel and airline bookings. You and your husband *will* be able to attend the gala awards ceremony next Saturday night?"

Gala event? Next Saturday? How had she missed that detail? Was it written somewhere in the fine print on their website? Oh well, better to get this all over with sooner rather than later.

"I'll be there." Brody on the other hand—that was another story. She highly doubted he would sanction her trip to New York, let alone accompany her. But she *could* take Charity if he chose to sulk.

"You will need to be in New York by next Friday afternoon," Rob continued, "so that your piece can be set up in the exhibition which opens to the paying public at ten on Saturday morning. Around midday, the judges will examine all fifty artworks and make their final decision on the winners."

"It is very possible that my husband might not be able to attend. If he doesn't, may I bring my daughter as my plus one? She's the girl in the field that I painted," Madison proudly announced.

"Absolutely!" Rob lowered his voice. "Don't tell your husband that I said this, but I do hope he's unavoidably detained because I'd love to have the opportunity to meet your muse."

Madison's soft chuckles melded with Rob's. "I'll see you next weekend then."

"I look forward to that," Rob said cheerily. "Oh, one more thing… I shouldn't be telling you this, but Ellie Sanders was really taken with your piece. I guess you know that she's a Kansas girl at heart, so it's not surprising that she would be predisposed to a piece from her home state, especially one exhibiting such talent. It's probably a good thing that there's a panel of judges choosing the final three winners, and not just Ellie."

"Definitely. I wouldn't want anyone to think that my entry got any special favor just because it depicted home for Ms. Sanders."

After saying goodbye, Madison ended the call.

She wanted to run upstairs to tell Charity, but she'd promised Sandy that she would be the first to know.

Seated behind his desk in his office at Peterson Galleries while Ava managed the floor, Brody tapped his fingers lightly over his laptop keys and stared at the sixteen-inch screen. He had promised Madison a special night, and he still hadn't managed to find anything to fit the expectation he'd created. It wasn't that there were no amazing places to stay—there were—but every time he found something, it had already been taken.

He leaned back in his chair and twined his fingers behind his head. He exhaled a long sigh to the ceiling then muttered, "That's what you get when you try booking a one-nighter at the last minute during summer vacation."

Not one to give up, Brody returned his attention to the Airbnb website. If he failed to find something, he'd resort to packing a tent and roughing it for the night. It's not as if they hadn't camped before. Still, he'd wanted to do something a little more special for his wife this time, keep the streak of peace and goodwill going strong.

The idea of postponing the night painting weekend flashed through his mind. No, not an option. Staying would mean having to go to church with Charity again. And he so needed a break from all of that. Squirming under conviction about his life every Sunday morning was something he did not relish. He could do without that for a few weeks. Or more.

Once again he typed Gove County along with Saturday's date into the search bar then scrolled through the familiar options. Maybe, just maybe, he had missed *some*thing.

He paused. *Wha—? No way.* How had he missed that beauty? Or had it perhaps not shown because it had been booked and was now visible due to a cancellation? He wasn't exactly sure how this reservation system worked. Didn't matter though—this place was perfect, and he was making a reservation and paying for it right away.

This was going to be fun, not to mention extremely romantic. Madison was going to love this place.

Who would've thought they'd be glamping? But it certainly did offer the best of both worlds as they could experience the quiet solitude of the great outdoors in comfort, style, and luxury.

Madison knocked on Charity's closed door. "Charity? Can I come inside?"

Getting no answer, she cracked the door open slightly and peeked inside.

Charity lay on her bed, one leg pitched in a V like a tent, the foot of her other leg resting on the arched knee. In her hands, she held a paperback. Headphones covered her ears—the source of her daughter's unresponsiveness. No doubt music blasted from the headset.

Baxter had curled up into a ball beside Charity. Poor puppy must be exhausted from playing with Charity and Melinda this afternoon if her knock hadn't stirred him.

She stepped closer and touched Charity's shoulder lightly.

Charity looked up and smiled.

She set her book down on the bed. Taking off the headphones, she shimmied up against her headboard.

Baxter stirred. He stretched his front legs out and slumped his head on her thigh.

"Hey, Mom, what's up? Did you finish your painting? Need help with something?"

Madison shook her head and sat down on the edge of the bed. "I'm done with the artwork. And yes, maybe in a little while you can help me with dinner?"

"Sure, Mom."

She took Charity's hand and squeezed it. "That's not why I'm here, honey."

Charity's eyes widened. "W–what is it? Is it Dad? Has something happened to him?"

"Cha—"

"Or you both? Are you getting a divorce?" Even though Madison had tried to interject, Charity's questions tumbled one after the other

Madison raised her voice. "Charity! Whoa!" She offered a smile. "Nothing is wrong, sweetheart. And everything's just perfect between your father and me."

But for how much longer?

"It is?" Charity clasped her chest. "Mom! Don't scare me like that again!"

"Well, if you had given me a chance to explain why I needed to talk to you before jumping to conclusions…"

Charity lifted her shoulders, her neck shortening with the action. She pursed her lips into a thin line then skewed her mouth to one side. "Sorry, Mom. So, what did you need to tell me?"

Madison drew in a deep breath, her pulse throbbing. Suddenly, doubts overwhelmed her. What if Charity wasn't happy that she'd entered her portrait into the contest? She should have asked her daughter's permission before doing so. It was, after all, no longer Madison's property. The painting belonged to Charity now.

Taking her daughter's hand once again, Madison raised her gaze to meet Charity's. "Honey, please don't be mad at me, but I…I entered your painting into a contest with Art USA. I–I hope you don't mind."

"Oh." Charity's brows lifted. "Sounds like quite a big contest. Is it national?"

"It is, honey. One piece from every state is chosen for the finals.

Not only is the prize money for the winner huge—it would certainly help fund some of your college education—but the opportunity for an exclusive exhibition at the Ellie Sanders Gallery in New York is priceless. Any artist given that break will be made for life. Art connoisseurs will line up to own a piece of that artist's work."

"Wow, sounds big. Of course I don't mind you entering the painting, as long as I get it back afterwards. It's a stunning piece, Mom, so I think you stand a good chance of winning."

Baxter lifted his head and gave Charity's hand a thorough lick.

She laughed, shifting her hand to rake her fingers through his silky coat. "What does Dad say about it? He must be excited at the prospects this could bring." Her breath hitched. "Does that mean we have to leave Cottonwood Falls? Move to New York?"

"No, honey, we're not moving anywhere. And...your Dad doesn't know I've entered."

Charity's eyes and mouth formed a perfect 'O'. Clamping her bottom lip between her teeth, she raised her brows again.

"I–I was mad at your father the day I entered. It's actually what spurred me on to enter. But even if I wasn't upset, I wouldn't have told him I was entering. I–I was afraid he might stand in the way. I thought it would be easier to just do it and ask for everyone's forgiveness afterward if I needed to. No point in telling anyone if nothing came of the endeavor. Right?"

Charity shrugged as she brushed soft puppy fur from her bedcover.

Baxter pounced on her hand with a loud yap, thinking it a game.

Charity moved her fingers across the cover again, chuckling as the pup retreated, butt in the air, tail wagging. He was gearing up for another spring, which came within seconds. "I just love this dog. He's so playful."

Drawing Baxter onto her lap, Charity tried to calm the puppy.

Her face grew serious. "You're absolutely right, Mom—Dad would've prevented you from entering, I'm certain. So I understand why you did what you did. You know, sometimes I can't help wondering if he's a little jealous of your talent."

A subdued laugh escaped Madison's mouth, and she cocked her head to the side. "Well, I don't know about that, but your father certainly does seem to have some sort of deep-rooted issues. Maybe one of these days he'll let me in on what his problem is." Although, if he hadn't done so after almost seventeen years of marriage, why would he say something now?

Realization dawned on Charity's face. "Wait just a minute... You said there was no point in telling anyone, unless... But you're telling me. Does this mean that—"

"Yes. I'm the finalist for Kansas." Madison beamed a smile.

"Mom, that's wonderful!" Charity flung her arms around Madison's neck and hugged her tightly. "I'm so proud of you. Will you tell Dad when he gets home?"

"Um, I think I should wait for the right time." Not that there would ever really be a right time with Brody. "Perhaps this weekend when we're out in the tranquility of the country. It might be easier to break the news to him gently in those surroundings. There's no telling how he'll react, so I'd like to make sure the waters are *really* smooth before I risk muddying them."

CHAPTER EIGHT

WHILE MADISON helped Brody pack the car with their art supplies and photographic equipment, Baxter bounced around Brody's feet, the laces on her husband's Converse All Stars a great source of entertainment for the pup.

Antsy with their new addition, Brody bellowed from the garage, "Charity, come and get your dog before I trip over him."

Within moments, Charity flew into the garage. "Sorry, Dad." She swooped Baxter up into her arms and rubbed his head. "Hey, you wanna go play ball out in the yard?"

Charity disappeared back through the door into the kitchen.

Madison returned her attention to carefully stacking a few blank canvases of varying sizes on top of their overnight bag and easels. She drew in a long, deep breath. It had been so much more difficult to keep the news of her win from Brody over the past forty hours or so than she had imagined it would be. Now that she knew she'd made it to the final fifty, she so badly wanted to tell him, wanted him to be proud of her achievement. But she couldn't say anything. Not yet. She needed a calm husband to hear the news, and at the moment, Brody was anything but. Before they returned tomorrow, however, she would need to come clean.

After dropping Charity and Baxter at Sandy's house, Brody steered the SUV west on Lake Road. Soon they were cruising down the K-150. In four and a half hours, with no stops, they'd reach their destination.

Despite several attempts to get Brody to spill the beans, he had refused to tell Madison where they were staying. All he'd said was that she needed to pack groceries to tide them over until lunch time tomorrow. And he'd bought four juicy rib-eye steaks—two for tonight she presumed, two for lunch tomorrow—unless somewhere along the line they were having company for one of their meals, which she doubted. They had no acquaintances in Gove County. If she didn't know any better, she'd hazard a guess that they were camping tonight. Except for one thing—Brody hadn't packed a tent or any bedding.

The day was warm and Brody soon cranked up the air-conditioning. The weather promised to peak at 93 degrees Fahrenheit in the late afternoon. Thankfully they'd only be going out to the rocks closer to 7 p.m., enough time to set up and start their artworks before the sun began to set nearly two hours later. If they didn't quite finish tonight, Brody would photograph the skies once it was dark so they didn't have to add the final touches to their canvases from memory.

The cool air blowing onto her face and feet, Madison smiled at Brody. "Thank you, honey. That feels way better."

"You're welcome. It was starting to get too hot in here." He shot her a flirtatious grin. "You have something to do with that?"

Madison's laughter filled the car. "Maybe." She held Brody's gaze for a moment before reminding him that he needed to keep his eyes on the road if he was to get them to Gove County in one piece.

One hand on the steering wheel, the other entwined in Madison's hand, Brody stared at the open road ahead, his shoulder-length hair dancing in the blast of air coming from the vents he'd turned to face him. "I forgot to tell you... Remember Marc Talbot, the artist from Burlington whose work we exhibited a few months ago?"

"I do. Extremely talented, but rather reclusive. Asked us to sell three stunning pieces, which were snapped up fast, earning us a quick and tidy commission." Madison shifted on her seat to face Brody. She reached out and tucked his hair behind his ear. "So what about him?"

"He stopped by the gallery yesterday morning. Said he was passing through Emporia and wanted to say hi. Anyway, it seems as if he's finding the confidence to put his art out there. Told me he'd entered the Art USA contest. He was hoping to hear by the close of business as it was the last day for winners to be notified. He showed me a photograph of the landscape he'd entered—a tornado ripping through the Kansas prairies. Stunning piece. I offered to exhibit it for him if he somehow didn't get into the finals."

Should she tell Brody about her entry now, seeing as he'd brought up the subject?

And spoil their night away?

No. Tomorrow was another day. No rush just yet.

"That's nice. Tell him I say hi the next time he's in the gallery." She rested a hand on his leg, giving it a light squeeze. "Do you mind if I catch a short nap? I didn't sleep very well last night, and as we'll have a late night tonight, I'd like to catch up on a little slumber."

"Knock yourself out, honey." Brody snorted. "Excuse the pun."

Brody's heart thrummed in his chest as he drove up the narrow, dirt track toward the large, corrugated iron barn with its barrel roof, grain silo, and hopper bin standing tall beside it. This place was certainly off the beaten track—nothing around for miles except wide open plains. Perfect for a romantic working weekend with his beautiful wife.

And bonus…the unique chalk formations with their many fossils that they'd come to immortalize on canvas, were merely a ten-minute drive away. He couldn't have chosen a better place.

Brody had first stopped at the owner's farm house, some three miles down the road to collect the keys to their accommodation. A lovely, middle-aged couple who told Brody and Madison that if they needed *anything*, they need only call.

Brody parked the SUV in the shade of a tall cottonwood tree close to the metal barn, and they clambered out of the vehicle.

As they rounded the car, concern creased Madison's features. Hand to her brow, she shielded her eyes from the glare of the midday sun and scoured the surrounds. "Um, so where exactly are we staying? We're in the middle of nowhere with nothing around except that old barn."

Brody chuckled and pointed to the barn. "There, babe. That's where we're staying."

Raising his arms, he stretched and arched his back, inhaling deeply of the fresh country air, the faint sweet, powdery smell of dried grains wafting on the breeze. He popped the hatch and released a satisfied sigh.

Madison burst out laughing. "Okay honey, joke's over. You're pulling my leg, aren't you?"

"Nope." Brody flashed her a grin then pulled the overnight bag out from beneath the easels and canvases. He set it down on the ground. "Nothing but peace and quiet here. Woo-hoo! What do you say we get this weekend started?"

Madison twisted around to examine the barn again. "In that case, if this really is where we're staying, I'd love to paint these buildings and fields. But later, when it's not quite so hot."

"Definitely. We could each tackle it from a different angle. And we have the whole of tomorrow to finish them off." Brody hadn't planned on getting two great locations to paint, but Madison was right. This place did deserve to find its way onto a canvas.

"Honey, bring the overnight bag. I'll carry the cooler and box of groceries inside."

Madison walked beside him as they headed toward the large, windowed, roll-up door that formed the front wall of the barn. "Let's just remember to make sure that the canvas sizes we choose can all fit in the SUV without touching one another. No stacking on top of each other going back home as we've done coming here."

"Thanks for the reminder. Wouldn't do to paint four *large* canvases—two of them would definitely need to be smaller in order to fit in the car without stacking."

"Absolutely."

Brody shot Madison a smile. "Seeing as you paint way faster than I do, you should tackle the two thirty-six by twenty-eight inch canvases, and I'll work on the twenty-two by sixteen inch ones. Sound okay?"

Madison nodded. "Sounds great."

Outside the silver-colored barn, two high-backed, slatted wooden chairs sporting bright red, yellow, and coral striped cushions stood beside the firepit which had been stacked with wood, ready to be lit. Brody's mouth salivated at the thought of those juicy rib-eyes sizzling over the hot coals. But he'd have to be patient—those were for dinner. Madison had packed wieners and buns for lunch. Hot dogs were the quick and easy choice after hours on the road.

Placing the cooler and grocery box down beside the roll-up door, Brody fished in his pants pocket for the key the owner had

given him. He unlocked the door then rolled it up, out of the way.

Luxurious finishes greeted them as they stepped through the wide opening. Wood-paneled walls—for insulation Brody assumed; a king-size four-poster bed with intricate carvings that matched the wooden bench at the end of the bed; and a thick, braided rug in the colors of a Kansas sunset, which extended out on all sides of the bed. Perched on a wooden cabinet close to the bed was a porcelain jug and basin. Brody suspected that was for winter visitors because the shower and two-person tub at this glamping spot was outdoors around the back, affording visitors the opportunity to bathe under the stars. Very romantic and definitely one of the selling points for him.

Madison dropped the overnight bag beside the table for two near the door. "Wow, this place is amazing—kind of where 'roughing it' meets 'going all out in style'."

"Exactly." Brody set the cooler down on the floor in the small kitchenette area, then slid the box onto the counter. "It's called glamping...glamorous camping. Get it?"

Madison laughed. "I get it. And I love it. Now *this* is my kind of camping, for sure." She flopped onto the bed and stared up at the silver curved roof. "Ooh, this is sooo comfortable."

She turned to look at Brody and patted the mattress beside her. "Come, try it."

Brody didn't have to wait for a second invitation from his wife to join her on a bed.

Lying down beside her, he leaned over. His hair fell across his face as he drew her into a kiss. Slowly and gently, his fingers fumbled with the buttons of her soft, silky blouse.

Madison's hand fastened around his to stop him. "The open door... Anyone can see inside."

A chuckle rumbled in Brody's chest. "Babe, they could see inside even if that door were closed. There are no blinds or curtains on that opening. I wouldn't worry though—there's nobody around for miles. Plus, I gave strict instructions to the owners when I made reservations that we were *not* to be disturbed under any circumstances. That's why they insisted we should call if we needed anything."

"W-e-l-l then, I guess as we'll have a very late night tonight, it would be a pity to waste the romance of this place."

Brody kissed her ear and whispered, "I do like the way you think."

Reluctantly, Madison eased out of Brody's arms. She threw back the white, Egyptian cotton sheet and rose, quickly finding her clothes.

"The bed to your satisfaction, my lady?" Brody propped himself up on his elbow, gazing at Madison as she buttoned her shirt. A lazy smile spread across his face.

"Very much." She turned and padded across the laminate wood floor to where Brody had left the cooler. "You hungry?"

"Starving. But only one dog or I'll spoil my appetite for that rib-eye. Only a few hours until dinner."

Multitasking in the small kitchenette, Madison packed the few items from the cooler into the small refrigerator. She set the coffee and tea containers on the counter, leaving the rest of the snacks in the box which she moved to the floor, out of the way against the wall. While the wieners heated, she cut and buttered the buns.

When the dogs where ready, Madison plated them then grabbed two pops from the refrigerator. Brody had just risen and dressed.

"You coming?" She headed outside, carrying the tray of food and drinks. She set it down on the firepit grid. "Now *that* makes a handy table."

"It sure does." Brody cracked open a can, grabbed a hot dog, and then sank onto the cushioned chair. "We'll have to bring the table outside later on though, because there'll be no using your makeshift table once the fire's roaring."

Madison grabbed her food and drink and relaxed into the chair as well. She closed her eyes for a moment and released a sigh before surveying the open plains. The sun warmed her face and she contemplated running inside to get her sunscreen and hat. "It's so beautiful and peaceful, I could stay here forever."

"Well, we do have the place until four tomorrow afternoon. I arranged a late checkout."

At least that would give her more time to find the right moment to tell Brody about Art USA.

After Madison had finished eating, she rose. "I'm going to take a quick shower before I make a start on painting this quaint landscape. Maybe tomorrow sometime you can relax in that chair for an hour so that I can paint you into the picture. I think it would be a great addition."

"For you, anything." Brody began to rise too.

"And where do you think you're going?" Madison asked.

Half out of his seat, Brody froze, holding her gaze. "You did say something about a shower…" Grinning, he waggled his brows.

She laughed. "Which I'm taking on my own. I do want to get *some* painting done this afternoon, and that might not happen if you join me."

Brody slumped back into his seat, dejected.

Madison pranced away, looking forward to a little alone time to gather her thoughts and start plucking up her courage.

By the time Brody had lit the fire and brought out the steaks later that afternoon, both he and Madison had made great progress with their barn and prairie paintings. He had fixed dinner because Madison had a much larger canvas to fill. Having the entire morning at their disposal tomorrow, they could easily finish their paintings. But just in case, Brody had made sure to photograph each of their views, as he always did. However, Madison's preference was to paint from real-time images.

From beside the firepit, Brody called to Madison. "I'm putting the steaks on the grill. Dinner will be ready in minutes. You might want to finish up for now and bring that canvas inside."

Madison nodded. She added the last brushstrokes of viridian green then carried the large canvas inside. She set it down beside Brody's smaller one, leaning it against the wood-paneled wall. Even though they'd chosen the same subject to paint, their artworks couldn't look more different, and not only because of the angles they'd chosen. Both Madison and Brody had opted to use the impasto technique, but whereas she had gone for applying the paint in a thick, bold fashion—loving the Van Gogh look with its brushwork so clearly visible—her husband's piece had more subtle textures, the strokes far more delicate.

Well, her canvas was way bigger. A whole lot more to do. But maybe subconsciously, she'd chosen the bolder approach, hoping it would psych up her courage. It hadn't worked. She was still just as nervous to tell Brody about Art USA. And she definitely did not want to tell him while they were out painting under the stars tonight.

Maybe later when they were in bed. Failing that, just before they left tomorrow.

Yes, that was probably the best possible time. At least that way if he did throw a hissy fit, she would only have to deal with his silence en route home. She was enjoying it out here far too much to risk spoiling their time together.

Dear Jesus,

I can't sleep. I can't stop thinking about Mom and Dad tonight. Has Mom managed to tell Dad about her win for Kansas? I'm so proud of her, and at the same time, so humbled that my painting won out of all the pieces that must have been entered from across our sunflower state. We have so many talented artists in our corner of the world, and so many awesome sights for those artists to depict in their work.

Please, Lord Jesus, give my mom the same measure of courage to tell Dad as you've given her talent. And please give Dad calmness and a sense of reasoning to accept the news Mom has. Let him be excited for her too.

With love
Your child
Charity

CHAPTER NINE

BRODY WOKE early to sunbeams trailing their silvery fingers through the glass roll-up door. He turned on his side to face Madison. She was still deep in dreamland. They had been so exhausted last night from the long session at Monument Rocks, having only returned after midnight, that they'd just washed their hands and feet and fallen into bed.

Exhaling a soft sigh, he rose, leaving Madison to sleep longer. He'd take a shower then tackle his landscape of the barn once again. He wanted to finish the artwork before they left this afternoon.

Under a steaming stream in the outdoor shower, Brody pondered their night. It had been amazing working beside Madison under such a breathtaking night sky as they painted those magnificent rocks onto their canvases. The dark surrounds had echoed with the calls of the Eastern screech-owl—more like a horse's whinny than the usual hooting sound owls made.

But as much fun as last night had been, Madison had seemed distracted, as if she had something weighing on her mind. Was it because he'd expressed a desire to join her in the shower yesterday afternoon, so soon after they'd made love? Did he come across as too demanding on her at times…in so many ways? It was just that he loved her so much and found her incredibly desirable. Often he feared he'd never get enough of her. But at the same time, he constantly fought his fears of losing her, just like—

No. He would not sully a beautiful day by allowing his thoughts to go down that rabbit hole again. Not today.

He shut off the water and smoothed the droplets from his hair and body before drying himself with a towel. Once dressed in shorts, a T-shirt, and his sneakers, Brody tied his hair back to keep it out of his way. Then he headed outside and set up his French easel in the same spot as yesterday. He returned to the barn for his canvas.

The sun had risen higher in the clear blue sky, and he'd made considerable progress on his painting, when his stomach rumbled. Maybe it was time to head back inside, whip up some breakfast, and wake his sleeping beauty.

He glanced away from the canvas toward the barn. Madison headed toward him, still dressed in her pajama top and shorts, a mug in each hand. She smiled and shouted, "I thought you might like a cup of coffee."

He set his brush down and closed the distance between them.

Madison placed a cup in his hand. "Good morning." She kissed him.

"Morning. And thanks for this. I was about to come inside to wake you and rustle up something to eat. Although I think it was rustle up breakfast first, then wake you."

"What time did you get out of bed?"

"Around six thirty. I took a shower then came on out here while the air was still cool and fresh." Brody took a long drink of the hot liquid. He smacked his lips together. "Ah, that's good." He hadn't wanted to turn on the coffee maker earlier for fear of disturbing Madison.

"Why didn't you wake me?"

"You were sleeping like a baby, and you know the old saying…let sleeping babes lie."

Madison eyed him over the rim of her mug. "I believe the correct wording is let sleeping dogs lie."

Brody shrugged. "Babies…dogs…same principle. When someone, or something, is sleeping, just leave it or them alone to enjoy their rest."

"Same principle, totally different meaning between using babies or dogs in that sentence." A soft laugh floated from her open smile.

Favoring the more creative arts at school, English grammar had never been Brody's strong point.

He grabbed Madison's free hand. "Do you want to see how I've progressed?"

They walked across to where the easel stood firm in the knee-high grass.

For a moment Madison quietly examined his work. Eyes twinkling with pride, she said, "I love it. You've done an amazing job with your technique. This will fetch a tidy sum once it's finished."

Brody slid his arm around her waist and pulled her into a hug. "Your approval means the world to me, you know that. And you've done a pretty nice job of your piece too."

Jaw dropping, Madison raised a brow and smacked his chest lightly. "Pretty nice job? I've done an amazing job, and you know it."

He leaned his forehead against hers. "You know I'm only messing with you. You *have* done an amazing job. Incredible in fact."

"And now I'm going to show you what an amazing job I can do of breakfast." Brody steered her back toward the barn's large entrance. "Why don't you hop in the shower, while I fix us a hearty meal?"

"I think I'll do that, if you don't mind cooking." Releasing his hand, Madison turned to go.

"I don't mind at all. And by the way…"

Madison twisted back, her eyes questioning as she waited for him to finish his sentence.

Brody smiled. "You've still got indigo streaks on your cheek and your fingers."

She lifted her hands to examine her fingers. Her brows drew together in a frown. "I don't have paint on my fingers…"

His smile widening to a grin, Brody snapped his fingers and pointed at her. "Got ya."

By the time Madison returned, rubbing her wet hair with the towel draped around her neck, Brody had just turned off the two-burner stove. He allowed his gaze to appreciate her attire for a moment—denim cut-off shorts and a white, off-the-shoulder, cotton blouse that only just touched the top of her shorts. With just the two of them out here and another scorching day forecast, he fully approved of her choice of clothes.

"You look cool." He plated the eggs beside the toast and bacon.

"I feel it." Madison sashayed closer. Fingers hovering over one of the plates for a second, she gave in and pinched a small piece of bacon between her fingers. She dropped it into her mouth.

Nodding her approval, she chewed then swallowed. "Hmm, tastes so good. I didn't realize how hungry I was until now."

Brody set the plates and coffee on the tray then carried it outside to where he'd set a table for two under one of the nearby Cottonwood trees.

"You've been busy setting all this up." Appreciation glowed in her eyes.

"I wanted to make this whole weekend special for you."

After transferring the coffee cups and plates to the table, Brody leaned the tray against the tree's large trunk.

Madison sank into her chair and lifted her knife and fork. She sighed. "Starting a day like this, it can only get better."

The thoughts he'd had of asking her if something had bothered her yesterday, dissipated with that single sentence. He didn't want to risk spoiling what promised to be a perfect day with his wife. If something really was bothering Madison, and it was really important, she'd tell him when she was ready.

Despite the time spent enjoying their late breakfast and later a lengthy lunch, both Brody and Madison finished their paintings of the barn by the time they needed to pack the car. The artworks of the Monument Rocks they'd started last night, they would finish back home in their studio.

Flattening the seats in the back of the SUV, Brody carefully positioned the wet canvases on the flat surface. Their overnight bag, cooler, camera bag, tripod, and French easels were tucked in the legroom behind their seats. Brody made sure to wedge the canvases tight. Unless he managed to flip the vehicle somehow, they wouldn't budge. They'd done this often enough, he had the drill down pat.

Leaving the key to the barn beside the kettle on the kitchenette counter as arranged, Brody pulled the windowed roll-up door shut then returned to the car where Madison waited. He slid onto the leather driver's seat then leaned over to Madison and drew her into a kiss.

"That was fun," he said. "We need to do that again soon."

"The kiss? Or the work overnighter?" A faint smile brushed her lips, not quite reaching her eyes before she glanced away.

"Both."

Wrapping one hand around the steering wheel, Brody turned the key in the ignition before he was tempted to stay another night. The engine roared to life.

Madison's mood was subdued on the trip home. After two hours of sporadic idle conversation, Brody finally decided to ask her if something was bothering her, if he'd done something to upset her.

Staring wide-eyed at him, her bottom lip quivered and her eyes moistened.

Brody's gaze darted between the road and Madison. Clearly, something was up.

Clamping her lip between her teeth in an obvious attempt to still the tremors, Madison closed her eyes and drew in a deep breath. "You've done nothing wrong, Brody. Yesterday and today...they were wonderful. But I— I have something I need to tell you."

He knew it. He knew something had been bothering her since yesterday.

She placed a hand on his leg, tightening her clasp. "Oh, please, don't be mad at me. Just hear me out."

His pulse began to race. Sounded more serious than he'd thought.

"Go on..."

"I–I entered the A–Art USA c–contest." Madison blinked as she stared at him. Was she waiting for a response? Well, he'd give her one all right.

"You did what?" It was impossible to keep the thunder from his voice. Especially because— "The same contest that I, only yesterday, mentioned Marc Talbot had entered?"

She swallowed hard and nodded, her bottom lip quivering.

"Why didn't you say something then, Madison?"

"I–I wanted to, truly, b–but I didn't want to spoil our weekend."

"Well, you've done so now. Congratulations." Sarcasm rolled off his tongue with that single word. Nostrils flaring, his breathing labored in long, deep inhales and exhales. "There's more to this, isn't there? Why are you telling me this now, unless—?"

"I took the win for Kansas." Madison attempted a smile but her mouth didn't seem to want to cooperate.

"Why didn't you tell me? Why didn't you first ask me what *I* thought about you entering before you went ahead and just did it?" He couldn't stop the brusqueness in his voice, and he didn't want to.

Madison drew her lips into a thin line. She looked away and gazed out of the side window. "I–I was afraid you'd prevent me from entering."

"Quite right I would've. And with good reason."

She slowly twisted back to face Brody, the look on her face and in her eyes bearing a little more boldness. "Really? And what *good* reason would that be?"

He couldn't tell her—couldn't talk to *any* of his family about his past. What if they all rejected him? All walked away? Like *she* had?

"Why wouldn't you be excited at the prospect of winning fifty thousand dollars, not to mention having the opportunity of an exclusive exhibition at one of the most renowned galleries in New York City? Being endorsed by Ellie Sanders…that would put our gallery on the ma—"

Brody thumped his hand against the steering wheel. "I. Said. No!" He should pull over to the shoulder and stop the car, before he flipped the vehicle over. But all he wanted was to get home and out of this enclosed space with Madison. She'd betrayed him. She'd lied to him. So instead, Brody kept the wheels rolling far too fast down the US-56, his gaze flitting between his wife and the asphalt.

"No?" Madison huffed, her eyes challenging. "I *can* make my own decisions on my career, Brody. You don't own me. Besides, it's all *your* fault I entered."

Incredible. Blame it on me.

He snorted. "My fault?"

"Yes. If I hadn't been so mad at you for taking off into the storm with Charity..."

Were these the same words his father had once listened to? Was history repeating itself?

Well, he wasn't going to take the fall for Madison's poor choices. "Oh, honey, admit it—you would've entered that contest whether I was in the dog-house or not." Bitterness tainted his words.

She opened her mouth, then shut it.

"And what artwork did you enter, because anything at the gallery belongs to Peterson Galleries, not you. As such, you would have no right to enter said piece. I could and should make you retract your entry."

Her gaze narrowed. "In that case, it's a good thing I entered *Girl in a Field*."

"*Girl in a Field*?" They didn't have any pieces by that title. Realization dawned. No way... She didn't... She couldn't have... "You entered *Charity's* birthday gift? Does she even know?"

"Yes, she does. So there is nothing you can do to make me pull my entry from the contest." Looking away once more, Madison said, "I'm leaving for New York on Friday. I would love nothing more than to have you at my side during the gala awards ceremony, supporting me, cheering me on... But if you don't come, I'll take Charity in your place."

"*You* are not taking *my* daughter anywhere. If you go to New York, Madison..." He sighed, then bulldozed on, "Don't bother coming back to Cottonwood Falls.

"Or me."

CHAPTER TEN

STARING OUT of the car's window, Madison fought back her tears as silence descended. They'd shared so much in the past two days—how could Brody forget so quickly? How could he let that all be clouded by the shroud of anger, bitterness, and resentment? She kept waiting, hoping, that Brody would talk to her…apologize… But he seemed resolved not to.

Then again, *she* had turned her back on him and chosen to ignore him for the rest of their journey. Even so, Madison couldn't believe that Brody hadn't had a kind word to say—not even the slightest hint of a congratulatory word or an nth of pride at her achievement. It was as if he wanted to keep her talent hidden in Peterson Galleries—like their gallery was to be the highest achievement of her career.

But to deny her the right to take Charity with her on a trip? Over her dead body. She was Charity's mother, and if Brody thought for a moment he could dictate what she could and couldn't do, he had better think again.

After an hour of deathly silence, Madison reached for her phone in the console where she'd stored it earlier. She turned her phone to vibrate and then texted Sandy. She didn't need Brody getting even more uptight at the incoming texts' chiming. And there were bound to be a few to and from her friend.

HEY THERE, CAN CHARITY STAY OVER AGAIN TONIGHT? TELLING BRODY ABOUT THE ART USA CONTEST DID NOT GO WELL. AFTER A WONDERFUL WEEKEND TOGETHER, WE'RE NOW NOT TALKING TO EACH OTHER. I DON'T WANT TO SUBJECT CHARITY TO AN EVENING OF THIS. THANKS. LOVE YOU.

Madison hit send. Gaze fixed on the screen, she waited for a response.

It didn't take long for the phone to vibrate against her palm. She opened the text and read.

THE JERK. I KNOW YOU LOVE HIM, MADS, BUT SOMETIMES I DON'T KNOW HOW YOU LIVE WITH HIM. I CAN'T BELIEVE HE'S UPSET WITH YOU. NO, SCRAP THAT, I CAN. IT'S BRODY PETERSON WE'RE TALKING ABOUT HERE. OK, RANT OVER. OF COURSE CHARITY CAN SLEEP HERE…FOR AS LONG AS SHE NEEDS. YOU TOO, IF IT COMES TO THAT. BUT I HOPE YOU CAN BOTH WORK THROUGH THIS QUICKLY, FOR ALL YOUR SAKES. LOVE YOU TOO MY FRIEND.

Wondering if she dared type another message, Madison shot a quick glance Brody's way. His eyes were firmly fixed on the road. Had he even noticed she was on her phone?

THANKS, SANDS. I COULDN'T GET THROUGH TIMES LIKE THESE WITHOUT YOU. YOU'RE SUCH A GOOD FRIEND. CHAT LATER. I'LL KEEP YOU UPDATED.

Gripping the phone tightly, Madison was about to close her eyes and sleep the rest of the way when another incoming message buzzed, sending tingling sensations through her palm.

WHAT ARE YOU GOING TO DO ABOUT NEW YORK? IF YOUR HUBBY CAN'T SPOT A GOOD THING WHEN HE SEES IT, I'LL HAPPILY ACCOMPANY YOU TO THE GALA AWARDS.

Oh, Sandy. Her friend did make her laugh.

Madison typed again. She'd need to make this her last text

before Brody *did* notice and find yet another thing to be upset about.

THANKS. I'D LOVE TO HAVE YOU THERE, BUT I PROMISED THE SPOT TO CHARITY IF BRODY DIDN'T WANT TO GO. AS FOR WHAT I'M GOING TO DO? GIRL, NOBODY'S GOING TO STOP ME FROM GOING TO NEW YORK. AND I'M STARTING TO THINK THE SOONER I LEAVE, THE BETTER. THIS IS TOO HUGE AN OPPORTUNITY TO PASS UP. NOW I'D BETTER STOP TEXTING BEFORE BRODY GETS EVEN MORE ANNOYED.

Madison hit send then closed her eyes again. But sleep didn't come. Her mind churned over what she could have done better. If she'd discussed the contest with Brody first, could she have talked him into seeing the benefits of her entering? She doubted it, but now she'd never know if her husband would've come around. She'd certainly messed this up by not being honest and up-front initially. Then again, the outcome would probably have been the same even if she had. Maybe worse. She might never have entered, never have known her true potential to make it to the top. And if, after discussing it with him, she'd decided to defy Brody and enter, this fight would've been far worse.

Right... Like this could get any worse. Brody had basically told her their marriage was over, and she wouldn't get Charity. Surely he didn't really mean that? Surely those were merely words spoken in the heat of the moment?

Maybe by the time they got home, he'd realize what he'd said and beg for her forgiveness.

Although expecting Brody to then give his blessing for her to go to New York might be a stretch.

Reaching the outer limits of Cottonwood Falls, Brody slowed the SUV. Instead of continuing on straight toward their house, he turned the vehicle to the left. Oh no, he was going to Sandy's house to fetch Charity.

She had to stop him.

"Brody... I–I arranged for Sandy to keep Charity tonight. It's best I think...given the circumstances."

Brody's lips pursed as he contemplated her suggestion.

"Please, Brody. For Charity's sake, not ours. Let's not drag her into this fight. Not tonight." Madison reached out and touched his shoulder.

He flinched, and her hand fell away.

Without warning, he spun the car around. The tires squealed, contending with the hard, gray surface beneath them.

Once home, Brody parked the SUV in the garage, sandwiching the vehicle between Charity's Beetle on the left and Madison's Mini Cooper on the right. They emptied the car in silence. Besides the cooler and leftover groceries, Brody unpacked only his own belongings—the two canvases he'd painted, his easel, camera, and tripod—leaving Madison's things for her to carry in. Including their overnight bag. Probably rationalized that it contained more of her clothing than his.

After three trips inside, Madison had her easel and two wet canvases safely stored in the studio. She returned for the overnight bag, her heart and mind a cauldron of broiling emotions. Anger, heartbreak, and fear all churned together, one of them threatening to boil over.

But which? Each would yield equally disastrous consequences.

Before she allowed her feelings to get the better of her, she would take a shower and head for bed. At least in slumber she could shout, scream, or cry.

Madison trudged upstairs to the bedroom. And it's closed door.

She turned the doorknob.

Locked.

Dear Jesus

93

So I'm sleeping over an extra night at Aunt Sandy's house. That can only mean one thing... Mom telling Dad about the contest did not go well.

I'm fearful for them, Lord. I'm so worried that this could be the fight they don't recover from. They're both so hard-headed at times. I know how much my mother wants this. And I can only imagine how much my father won't want her doing it.

I don't want their marriage to break up. I don't want to have divorced parents—maybe having no choice with whom I would stay. And even if I did have a choice, how could I favor one over the other? I love both of my parents equally. And I want them to grow old together.

Please, dear Jesus, help them to reconcile.

With love
Your daughter
Charity

(At least, with you, there is no fear of separation.)

94

CHAPTER ELEVEN

MADISON SHOT upright in bed, her body damp with a cold sweat, and not because the weatherman had forecast another scorching day in Kansas. She wiped her face with her palms, the vivid image fresh in her mind—Brody and her tugging at Charity's arms, their daughter's screams as her body began to rend in two.

Tucking her hair behind her ears, out of the way, she exhaled a weighted sigh and whispered, "It was only a dream...only a dream."

Although Charity's bed had been comfortable, Madison had not woken refreshed. When she finally turned the light out last night, sleep had not come easy. And by the time it did, her slumber was consumed with dark, disturbing dreams of her and Brody splitting up and the ensuing fights over Charity.

Madison threw back the covers and rose. She stared up at the *Girl in a Field* hanging on Charity's wall above her bed. She had locked the bedroom door last night, fearing that Brody might just sneak in and steal that painting off the wall. She'd put nothing past him sabotaging her being in New York with that canvas this weekend.

She unlocked the door then padded down the passage to her

own bedroom. Unlike last night, the door now stood wide open. She tiptoed inside.

Empty, the bed made as if it hadn't even been slept in.

Was Brody downstairs, or had he already left?

She glanced at the digital clock on the nightstand. Six forty-five. Brody usually headed for Emporia around seven-thirty. He must still be downstairs. Had the night apart helped his temper to cool? She could only hope so.

One way to find out...

Madison turned and exited the bedroom.

The kitchen was silent, deserted. Madison poked her head inside the garage. Brody's SUV was gone. So he had left for work way earlier than normal, without saying goodbye or leaving a note.

Well if that was the way he wanted to play this, she knew exactly what she needed to do next—be away from the situation so that Brody could have time to calm down. And staying here in the house wouldn't help him to change his mind. All it would do was enflame the situation. With her gone, hopefully he'd miss her and see how foolish he'd been. Perhaps that would spur him on to join her in New York before Saturday night.

She headed to the office and fired up her laptop. An email had come in over the weekend from Robert Morris containing suggested flights from Kansas City to New York on Friday, returning on Sunday. Well that wouldn't work.

She opened Expedia and booked two flights to New York—one for herself, one for Charity. Once Madison received the confirmation email, she replied to Rob's mail.

Dear Rob,

Thank you for the suggested travel itinerary. Something has come up, and I will be flying to New York this afternoon. I've already booked my flights. My daughter, Charity, will be attending the gala event with me. Please do go ahead and book the hotel room for Charity and me for Friday and Saturday night.

Madison didn't know how involved the artists would be once setting up for the event and exhibits commenced, so she'd rather be close on hand at the hotel than at her parents' house.

We'll see you sometime on Friday, then—me, Charity, and the Girl in a Field.

Regards

Madison

She hit send then grabbed her laptop and shoved it into its bag along with the power cord. She slung the bag over her shoulder then returned to the kitchen for a quick bowl of cereal. With her flight at 6 p.m., she didn't have the entire day to prepare. She and Charity would need to leave by two at the latest. Her day would be really full—she needed to pack for both of them and wrap the painting for safe traveling. Only then could she head over to Sandy's to fetch her daughter. Plus, she'd need to find time to carefully explain to Charity what she was doing and why. Hopefully she would understand and agree to accompany Madison to New York for the week.

After she'd eaten breakfast, Madison retrieved two suitcases from the garage. She took them upstairs and set one down on Charity's bed.

In her own bedroom, she sorted through the clothes on her shelves and hangers, choosing wisely for the New York humidity. When she had packed her suitcase, Madison moved on to her sweet girl's room. If she left packing that suitcase up to her daughter, there'd be only shorts and T-shirts in that suitcase. Charity did need a beautiful dress for the gala awards.

Madison folded the peach-colored, sixteenth-birthday dress worn merely a month ago and placed the soft fabric at the top of some well-chosen outfits. She added the white cotton dress her daughter had worn when she sat—or rather stood—for the portrait.

The soft sound of music tinkling from the back pocket of her jeans made Madison pause.

Heart thudding, she reached into her pocket. Could it be Brody calling to apologize?

She shot a glance at the screen, her heart freefalling in disappointment.

"Hey, Sands, I was about to call you." Well, it *was* next on her to-do list once she'd packed Charity's bag.

"How are things in the Peterson household?" her friend asked, her voice dripping with empathy.

"Terribly quiet." Madison sighed and sank onto her teen's bed. "Brody must've left at least an hour early this morning."

"What?" Sandy's pitch rose. "And that after locking you out of your bedroom last night? He really is pulling out all the stops to avoid you. How are you supposed to sort this nonsense out if you don't see your husband?"

Madison pursed her lips and shrugged, not that Sandy could see her doing so. "I'm not."

"You're what?" Confusion laced Sandy's two words.

Eyes stinging, Madison blinked back the tears that threatened and swallowed hard. "I'm not going to sort this out. At least, not now. I–I'm leaving for New York this afternoon, and I'm taking Charity with me."

"Whoa, Madison... More power to ya, girl! I'm so glad you're not backing down and letting this opportunity pass you by. You'll always wonder if you don't see this through to the end. And you'll always resent Brody for that too."

Sandy was right. Madison *would* hold this against Brody if she didn't pursue her win, see where it could lead for Peterson Galleries. Besides, he was being totally unreasonable. And he gave no reason why he hadn't wanted her to enter.

"But, you're leaving so soon? Don't you only need to be in New

York by Friday night?"

"I–I can't stay here until then, Sands…drag Charity into this mess. And I'm hoping that with both me and Charity away, Brody might miss us and rethink his actions." Maybe even apologize for the way he'd treated her, the things he'd said. But how many bottles of perfume, or boxes of chocolate, or dozens of roses did a girl need when all she wanted was her husband's support, respect, and understanding?

"I'll visit my parents until Friday, stay at the hotel Friday and Saturday night, and then back to my parents' house for Sunday night. I've booked flights home on Monday afternoon."

A soft whistle floated through the phone. "Five nights with your folks… You *must* be desperate to get away."

A chuckle slid from Madison's lips. "W-e-l-l…that aside, Charity does need to spend some time with her grandparents. Why not now while she's still on summer break?"

Madison rose and tucked the phone between her shoulder and ear so that she could continue packing Charity's bag.

"Because, um, the timing," Sandy said. "*And* the fact that you probably haven't told your husband about your plans. I'm concerned, Mads, that this could all blow up in your face."

Madison was also worried, but she wouldn't tell anyone that. She had to take a gamble that by leaving Brody, he would see that he didn't mean what he'd said when he told her if she went to New York not to come home.

She cleared her throat. "W–would you mind terribly keeping Baxter until we return? I can't leave him here alone all day."

"Of course I'll keep the pooch. Melinda will be excited. She's grown rather fond of young Baxter. So much so, I may need to get a puppy in the house too."

Madison heaved a relieved sigh. "Thanks, Sandy."

"Meh, no big deal. Besides, that's what friends are for. Right?"

Madison could see Sandy jutting out that sharp chin of hers and raising her pixie nose with that last word.

"*You* go above and beyond, my friend. One day, you're going to make another lucky man very happy." If only Sandy would give love another chance.

Sandy drew in a breath so deep, Madison could hear it through the phone. "I don't know about that. Grant was my soulmate."

"And you don't think you can have another in life?" Madison's thoughts flashed to what *her* life would be like without Brody. Would she ever be able to fall in love again if anything were to happen to him…to them? Still… "Grant has been gone for six long years, Sands. One of these days, I'm going to make it my life's mission to help you to find someone worthy of your love."

Sandy chuckled. "Or die trying?"

"Exactly." Madison's gaze scanned Charity's dresser to see what else her daughter would want packed. Brush, makeup, hairspray… That should about do it. Anything she'd forgotten, she'd buy in New York.

"Mads, would you like me to drop Charity later?"

"It's okay. If you don't mind, soon as I'm done here, I'll come on over. I want to get out of this house as soon as I can, just in case Brody decides to return." He'd been married to her for long enough to suspect she might leave for New York earlier. "I'm almost done packing, then I just need to package the painting for transporting to New York. I'll see you in two hours max."

"Great. And a good idea to get out of the house. What time is your flight?"

"Six p.m. Probably best I leave around two. Traffic to MCI can sometimes be delayed, especially as one gets into the airport."

"Sounds good. I'll make lunch for 1 p.m. so you can be on the road by two, because if I know you, you'll get so busy and distracted with everything today, you'll totally skip food."

Her friend knew her so well.

"Deal." Madison said goodbye and focused on Charity's suitcase. She would find the right time on the way to the airport to explain fully to Charity why they were leaving so suddenly.

CHAPTER TWELVE

IF ANYONE had asked Madison yesterday morning if she'd be taking a trip to New York this afternoon, she would've laughed.

What a crazy, blue Monday, she mused as she steered her red Mini Cooper down the I-35 N, the back seat crammed with her and Charity's overflow luggage, not to mention the boxed canvas standing behind the front seats. Usually they'd make a trip to the airport in Brody's SUV—as a family. Having to do so in her small vehicle… Well, all she could say was that it was a good thing she only had Charity in the car beside her, because the trunk was too small to fit both of their suitcases plus Charity's backpack and their carry-on bags.

The trip to Kansas City airport had started with great excitement, Charity recalling their last visit to New York for her thirteenth birthday and everything she, Madison, and Brody had done together. A visit to the Statue of Liberty and the 9/11 Memorial. A leisurely stroll through Central Park. Looking down on the sprawling city from the heights of the Empire State Building, as well as from the Top of the Rock—the observation deck on the 70th floor of 30 Rockefeller Plaza. Those were just a few of the highlights.

That had been their last visit to New York City. Since then, life had been too busy, the demand for her artwork increasing year after year. Besides, Madison's parents always made sure they visited at least two or three times a year, so the need to make the journey to the Big Apple was never pressing.

When they neared Emporia, Charity asked if they could stop by the gallery, but Madison tried to get her to see reason. Brody would, no doubt, try to prevent them both from going and she couldn't handle yet another ugly scene. It was necessary for them to be away from home until Brody calmed down.

"But Mom, I didn't even get to say goodbye, and I haven't seen Dad since Saturday," Charity argued. "We're going to be away for an entire week."

"I know, honey, but trust me. This is for the best, as I've already explained."

They settled into conversation about all kinds of things, except Brody. They'd just passed Ottawa when Charity turned to Madison. "Mom, are we really doing the right thing?

Shouldn't you have rather waited until Friday? Dad might've changed his mind by then and joined you." Uncertainty clouded her big, blue eyes, so like her father's.

Madison shook her head. "I highly doubt it. I've been married to your father long enough to know how he will and won't react. I can honestly say that this will take him some time to get over." She just hoped that by the time they got back home to Cottonwood Falls, he had—*and* that he'd forgiven her for entering the contest and going to New York without him, taking their daughter instead.

"Crazy thought, Mom. What if Dad also entered the contest and was bitterly disappointed when you told him that you'd taken the win for Kansas, realizing he'd failed? It *could* explain his strange behavior." Charity scrunched her nose, shifting the freckles that dotted her skin. "I've always thought Dad was maybe just a tiny bit jealous of your talent."

Crazy thought?

Brody entering Art USA certainly wasn't something Madison had considered. But surely he wouldn't have? Unlike her, he would've said something.

She turned and offered Charity a wobbly smile. "I–I don't think so, honey—that he entered or that he's jealous of me." But Madison's words were more to reassure herself than her daughter.

The day at the gallery had been long—especially as he'd arrived forty-five minutes early—so Brody was relieved when he was finally able to lock up shop, get into his SUV, and cruise the familiar US-50 west back to Cottonwood Falls. Although he wasn't looking forward to facing Madison.

Still, so often today he'd wanted to pick up the phone and call her, tell her he was sorry, that he didn't mean the awful things he'd said yesterday. But he couldn't, even though he had desperately missed the feel of her next to him last night and the sound of her voice this morning. It was the first time he'd ever locked her out of their bedroom. But one day, hopefully, she would see that the stance he'd taken was for her own good.

For *their* own good.

How is she supposed to know that if you won't tell her?

Right… If only he could open up to her. But he'd never been that vulnerable with anyone before. And if he confided in Madison, would she keep the secret he had carried alone for decades? What if she told Faith? And Faith told Tyler? He shuddered to think what his "family" would think of him then? His siblings would probably resent him for fooling them for a lifetime.

And most importantly, how would Madison react to this hidden part of his life?

Hopefully she would have had a change of heart about this contest by the time he got home. How he longed to hear her say that she was sorry she'd gone behind his back, that she'd be pulling out of the contest. If he were a praying man, he'd be down on his knees right now asking God for exactly that. But his wife could be so hard-headed at times that it wouldn't surprise him in the least if she'd already booked her ticket to New York for Friday. Or contacted "Daddy" to fly his private jet to Emporia to fetch her.

Then again, she could be so unpredictable too. Maybe she would surprise him—in a good way.

Brody arrived home just after six, as he always did. He pressed the remote control dangling from his keyring. The large, wooden garage door began to roll up. Like a ray of sunshine, Charity's bright yellow Volkswagen greeted him.

Strange, Madison's car wasn't there. She was probably over at Sandy's house.

After parking, Brody stepped inside the house.

"Charity…"

Deathly silence greeted him, like an unwanted guest. Not even a yap from Baxter. Where was that pooch?

He set his briefcase and jacket down on the kitchen counter then gave a soft whistle, expecting any minute to see Baxter round the corner and burst through the open door, claws clicking like castanets against the floor tiles.

Nothing.

Had Madison taken Charity *and* Baxter with her? For a simple visit to her friend, assuming that's where she was? Didn't those girls realize that the dog *could* survive for a few hours at home alone.

Brody strolled over to the stove and opened the eye-level oven door. He drew in a deep breath then slammed the door shut. The only thing simmering in this kitchen was his annoyance.

He yanked his cellphone from his shirt pocket and dialed Madison's number, ready to give her an enormous piece of his mind.

You've reached Madison. If you're listening to this message, I'm probably up to my pigtail in canvases and paint. So leave your name and number, and I'll get back to you as soon as I can.

Annoyed, Brody hung up without leaving a message.

He tried Charity's number.

Hey, it's me. You know what to do after the beep. Beeeep. His daughter's giggle followed before voicemail kicked in.

"Charity! It's your father. Call me. Or tell your mother to call me."

Brody opened the refrigerator then poured himself a glass of fruit juice. Then he took out the cheese and cut himself a thick slice. Munching the cheese and sipping the juice, he headed upstairs. He'd have a shower first, and then worry about whether he'd have to rustle up his own dinner.

His irritation fractionally tempered after he'd freshened up, Brody dressed, leaving a smaller towel around his neck until his hair dried. He lifted his phone from where he'd discarded it on the bed.

Nothing.

Neither Madison nor Charity had returned his calls.

He dialed Sandy's number.

After several rings, Sandy answered. "Brody…"

Annoyed with Sandy by default, Brody forced a pleasant tone to his voice or else he'd get nothing out of Madison's best friend.

"Sandy, hi. Are Madison and Charity perhaps at your place?"

"Nope."

A short and not-so-sweet answer. But what else had he expected from Sandy? Madison had probably told her everything about their fight.

"Um, well, do you know where they might be?" he asked, still remaining cordial.

"Maybe."

Good grief. Hell might have no fury like a woman scorned, but the best friend of such a woman had just as much fire in her.

"Well, could you tell me then? I'm worried about my wife and daughter."

"Humph," came Sandy's one-syllable response.

Brody had to bite his tongue not to tell her what an absolute bundle of joy she was tonight…a woman of many, many words.

"Sandy, please, if you know where they are, I need to know." He wasn't begging, but if it took sounding like that to find out where Madison and Charity were, then so be it.

"They're on a plane to New York," Sandy spat. "And I don't blame them one bit!"

It was dark and late by the time Madison and Charity stepped off the plane at LaGuardia Airport. Would've been so much easier if they'd been able to fly into Newark airport. Oh well, at least their return flight was from there, so much closer to her parents' Staten Island home.

They each grabbed their suitcases from the luggage carousel then stacked them and their carry-on bags onto a baggage cart. Madison carried the narrow, rectangular box with the canvas safely tucked inside—'Handle With Care' labels stuck on both sides—while Charity pushed the cart.

Out in the arrivals area, a good-looking, uniformed man around Madison's age held a board with Madison & Charity written on it. Spotting them, he smiled and headed their way.

He held out a hand. "Hello, I'm William, but you can call me Liam. Your father sent me to fetch you."

Shaking his hand, Madison said, "Hi. I'm Madison Peterson and this is my daughter, Charity." She smiled. "Thank you so much for picking us up, especially this late."

Liam tipped his chauffeur's cap. "It's my pleasure, Mrs. Peterson." He took the baggage cart from Charity.

Just over an hour later, her father's Lincoln Town Car pulled up outside her parents' elaborate, Queen Anne-style home. She had grown up in a house only slightly less stately than this one that bordered the Saint Francis Woodlands. Madison could never understand why her parents wanted to go bigger and fancier once her father made it to the top of the corporate ladder. Especially as it was just the two of them, and the place they'd previously lived in more than showed off their achievements.

Status and success—it made people do crazy things.

Like entering art contests without their husband's knowledge?

She pushed the convicting thought aside. Besides, she hadn't entered to achieve status, to be able to flaunt her success to the world. She'd done it for their gallery. At least that's what she kept telling herself. If she won, the exposure would be invaluable for Peterson Galleries.

Tired from the long day and the unresolved turmoil between her and Brody, Madison stepped through the front door. She leaned the protected canvas against the wall beside the entrance then fell into her father's embrace.

"Daddy, thanks for sending a car to fetch us." Even though he could be a stuck-up, stick-in-the-mud at times, she'd always felt safe in her father's arms.

Her heart constricted. She'd always felt safe in Brody's arms too.

Until now.

"Madison..." Father gave her a tight squeeze then opened one arm to pull Charity into the hug. "Charity... It's so good to see you girls again, although I must admit that your call earlier this afternoon was rather a surprise. I'm intrigued to hear what has so suddenly brought you both to our part of the world for a week."

"I'll fill you in once Mother is with us," Madison said.

Father's thick, gray brows quirked. "I'm afraid that'll only be in the morning. Your mother asked me to offer her apologies that she's not here to greet you. She needed to retire early. But she said to tell you that she would see you at breakfast. She had a very busy afternoon today at a fundraiser, and mid-morning tomorrow she has another charity event which she must attend. I believe there's one more at the end of the week, so it seems you won't see that much of her." Father chuckled, his gaze drifting to the wrapped painting against the wall. His mouth curved in a smile. "A gift for your mother and me?"

Madison shook her head. "Not this time, Daddy. I'll explain later."

She turned to the driver. "Liam, you can leave our bags just inside the door. I'll get them upstairs in a little while."

Tiny lines furrowed Liam's forehead. "I would never think of leaving you to lug these heavy suitcases upstairs, Mrs. Peterson."

He turned to his employer. "Sir, with your permission..." His gaze traveled up the ornate staircase.

"Of course, William. Just place the suitcases against the wall on the landing. My daughter and granddaughter are quite capable of wheeling their luggage from there."

Tipping his head, Liam wrapped his fingers around Madison's suitcase and her smaller carry-on bag—one piece of luggage in each hand. He glanced at her. "I'll be down in a minute to get your daughter's bags."

With a nod, Father ushered Madison and Charity toward the kitchen. "Are you girls hungry?"

Madison shook her head. "We had a rather substantial lunch at

Sandy's house. And then a snack on the plane. Besides, Daddy, it'll soon be midnight. Time for bed, I'd say."

Pausing in his stride, father grinned as he splayed his palms toward the ceiling. "And *that* is why I like to travel in the company jet. It's faster, and you don't have to get home at a ridiculous hour. You really should've called me this morning, Madison. I could have had my pilot fly to Emporia to fetch you."

Madison rolled her eyes. "Don't be silly, Dad. That's totally unnecessary and far too extravagant." It might be fine for her parents, but she didn't have a problem flying with a commercial airline.

Charity gripped Madison's arm. "What? Mom... Next time, take Grandpa up on his offer. That would certainly beat flying coach."

"Goodnight, Sir," Liam called from the large hallway.

They all turned to acknowledge him.

"Goodnight, Liam."

"Goodnight, William." Her father's voice lagged behind hers and Charity's, his sentence a syllable longer.

Once again, the charming chauffeur tipped his cap. "Mrs. Peterson...Charity... Have a pleasant stay, although I'm sure we'll cross paths again before I return you to the airport next Monday."

The front door clicked as he exited.

"He seems very nice," Madison said. "Way younger than the last chauffeur you had, though. How long has he been working for you?"

"William?" Her father's brow furrowed.

No, Dad. The man in the moon. Of course your chauffeur.

"He's been with me for about a year now. A very pleasant fellow indeed."

Father pointed toward the kitchen. "Are you sure I can't get you something to eat, or drink. And where is Brody? Why didn't he travel to New York with you?"

"Who would look after the gallery, Daddy?" Not wanting to get into a discussion about Brody right now, Madison deflected the conversation from her husband. "Dad, I'd love to sit and chat over a coffee, but right now, Charity and I are both really tired. It's been a long day. We can talk further over breakfast, okay?"

She kissed her father's cheek then lightly grasped Charity's elbow. "Come along, sweetheart."

Charity nodded and pecked her grandfather's cheek. She took a step to follow Madison then paused. "Grandpa, will you show me around the house tomorrow morning? This place is awesome, and way bigger than the one I visited last time."

Lips parting, her father smiled. "It would be my pleasure. But it'll have to be early, before breakfast. William picks me up around seven fifteen to take me to the office, so I'll meet you in the kitchen bright and breezy?"

Charity's head gave a slight bob. "Six thirty?"

Father's shoulders shook with his chuckle. "Only if you want me to miss breakfast. Rather make it five thirty. This house is a lot bigger than it might look."

Charity grinned. "Deal."

Madison's brows drew together. "Sweetheart, that doesn't give you much time for sleep tonight."

"It's all right, Mom. Sleep's overrated anyway. Besides, I can always catch a powernap in the afternoon, or go to bed early tomorrow night. I'm itching to explore this house."

Madison blew out a sigh, too exhausted to argue. Seemed she couldn't win with anyone these days. Not her mother or her father. Not her husband. Not even her teenage daughter.

CHAPTER THIRTEEN

THREE DAYS was all it had taken for Madison to be relieved at moving to their five-star hotel in Manhattan for two nights. Charity felt the same way she was sure, although her daughter didn't say as much. Sometimes, Charity was just too polite—especially when it came to her grandparents.

Madison zipped her overnight bag shut then wrapped her fingers around the handle. With her other hand, she hefted the well-protected canvas underneath her arm and headed for her bedroom door. Of course, not hearing from Brody all week—he'd even been silent with Charity—compounded by her mother's perpetual caustic remarks about how Brody should be at the exhibition and ceremony tomorrow night, not only to show his support, but the gallery's too, hadn't helped warm Madison to any ideas of staying home for the weekend as well. As far as Mother was concerned, Brody's assistant should be quite capable of handling business at the gallery for a few days.

As Madison headed downstairs, her mother's voice surfaced in her memory.

"Don't worry, Madison dear. The moment you told us about your win for Kansas, I immediately cleared our calendars and pulled some strings to get seats at one of the tables for your father and me on Saturday night. They did not come cheaply, but anything to support our girl."

Madison and Charity's one saving grace for tomorrow night was that, according to Rob, the fifty finalists and their plus ones were placed together at tables of ten. This meant that her parents could be seated anywhere but at the ten VIP tables. Knowing her mother though, anything was possible. It wouldn't surprise Madison in the least if the great Virginia Harding-Forbes managed to secure a seat right beside Ellie Sanders.

Charity already waited at the front door, dressed in jeans, sneakers, and a soft, sleeveless chiffon shirt.

Madison perched her bag next to her daughter's, and then set the box down against the wall. Shouldn't be too long before Liam arrived in the sleek, silver sedan. She glanced around the spacious hallway, ears pricked for the sound of high-heeled shoes.

Nothing.

She turned to Charity. "I guess I'll have to go and find your grandmother so that we can say goodbye. She'll never forgive me if I don't, even though we'll see her and your grandfather tomorrow night." Not to mention being back in this house on Sunday morning.

The click-clack of heels against the tiled floor echoed through the house.

"She's coming," Charity whispered.

Their heads snapped to the right as Madison's mother rounded a corner and headed toward them.

At the same time, a knock sounded at the front door. Must be Liam.

"You get the door," Madison told Charity. "I'll deal with your grandmother." She pivoted and closed the distance to her mother who had paused beside a nearby console table to primp the flowers in a vase.

Mother turned to Madison. "I'm sorry to keep you girls waiting. I had some last minute details to attend to for the charity event at one. But by the look of things, it seems my timing is perfect." She gazed past Madison. "William, once you've dropped my daughter and granddaughter at their hotel, please hasten back. I need to be at the Grand Hyatt in Midtown Manhattan by midday."

Why her mother couldn't just drive with them now was beyond Madison. The Grand Hyatt wasn't far from their hotel. But heaven forbid Mother should arrive anywhere early—that was as bad as arriving late according to her mother. It wasn't as if she couldn't while away the time shopping, or drinking coffee at some trendy Manhattan coffee shop, or just hanging out with her and Charity.

And she wouldn't hear a thing about Madison and Charity going in a little later with her.

"Lose all that time in the car to go over my speech because the two of you won't be able to remain quiet for that long? No thank you. William can make the additional trip."

So the chauffeur would need to drive back and forth between Staten Island and Manhattan because what Mother wanted, she got.

With everything.

Madison glanced at the box containing her canvas. Well, almost everything.

If it wasn't for that package being rather cumbersome, Madison would've just clambered on a bus into the city with Charity.

If only Brody was here with them. He knew how to stand up to her parents. He would've insisted her father loan them one of his many cars for the weekend and driven them around himself. Madison steered clear of driving in this busy city. She was used to Kansas life, especially Cottonwood Falls, where the roads weren't bustling with cars like ants on a log drizzled with raw honey.

Her heart squeezed as she planted a peck on her mother's cheek.

She missed her husband terribly. Was this contest worth this heartache? Maybe she should just reroute Liam to Newark Airport and be done with all of this.

Charity hugged her grandmother. "Thank you for everything. Especially for having my laundry done daily."

Mother cracked a smile. "Well, darling, I do have to keep the maids busy."

As if this house wasn't big enough to keep the staff working from morning till evening.

"At least if we get home and my dad kicks us out, I'll have a suitcase bursting with clean clothes."

Groan. Why would Charity go and say something like that? Especially to her mother!

"Kick you out? Why on earth would your father do something like that?" Mother's gaze snapped to Madison. "What's going on, Madison?"

Madison drew in a deep breath, exhaling her words. "Nothing, Mother."

"Don't you nothing me, young lady. Are you two having problems? Is that why you're here without your husband?"

Like an answer to prayer, Madison's phone rang. She retrieved it from her handbag.

Robert Morris? Why would he be calling her now?

"I'm sorry, Mother. I need to take this. We can talk further on Sunday." Hopefully her mother would get the hint that this discussion was closed for now. Madison answered the call. "Rob. Good morning."

Rob's voice boomed through the phone. "Maddie. Morning. Are you ready and excited for tomorrow?"

"Yes. Of course," she said, even though only moments ago she'd been considering walking away from everything. "We were actually about to leave my parents' house. Thanks so much for arranging that early check-in."

"I'm glad to hear that," Rob said. "If it's okay with you, could I meet you at the hotel as soon as you've checked in? I'd like to take you, Charity, and the *Girl in a Field* down to the exhibition hall. I just got off the phone with Ellie, and she wants to see your exhibit ASAP. I think she has a prime spot in mind for her home state piece."

What? "O–of course. Meet us in the lobby around ten." Madison hung up.

"Madison…," Mother started.

What now? Was she going to press Madison again for information?

"Mom, I said Sunday. Charity and I need to go. Now! We're meeting the contest organizer in an hour and we still need to check into our hotel."

As she walked out of her parent's home and slid into the back seat of her father's car, excitement welled in Madison's breast, washing away any thoughts of giving up and returning home.

Madison was certain that Robert Morris had contacted the hotel after his earlier call to her, because their check-in had been smooth, effortless, and speedy.

She gazed at Charity with pride. "You look so beautiful, honey."

Charity huffed. "Really, Mom, do I *have* to wear this dress? Going around the city would be far easier and way more comfortable in the jeans and sneakers I *was* wearing."

Madison lifted a lock of Charity's hair and trailed her fingers down the thick strawberry-blond curl. "Please, Charity honey, humor me this once. I think it will make a huge impression on Ellie Sanders to see the real life *Girl in a Field* beside the immortalized

116

canvas one."

"All right... But I'm taking the clothes I had on earlier with me and changing the moment I can." Charity flounced over to the bed and began stuffing her jeans, sneakers, and blouse into her backpack.

The clock marching closer to ten, Madison hurried Charity out of their hotel room with one hand while clasping the rectangular box tightly under her other arm.

The moment they strolled into the hotel lobby, a tall, slender, forty-something man dressed in a stylish gray suit rushed toward them. Streaks of silver highlighted the hairline of his darker head—the result of working for a highly talented visionary artist and connoisseur?

He stuck out his hand in greeting. "Maddie… It's so good to finally meet you."

It had been easy for Robert Morris to recognize them thanks to Charity's dress and the large box with its red and white warning labels tucked under Madison's arm. Then of course, there was that headshot Madison had emailed to Rob last Friday.

He shifted his focus. "And you must be Charity."

Charity smiled as she shook Rob's hand. "Or *Girl in a Field*, if you prefer."

Rob chuckled. "Not only beautiful, she's sassy too. Although that didn't come across in your mother's painting which exudes innocence." He relieved Madison of the unwieldy box. "Shall we go?"

Madison nodded eagerly, and Rob led the way to the door.

"Do you mind walking to 30 Rockefeller Plaza?" he asked. "It's only a few blocks from here."

Madison tipped her head in agreement. "Of course not. The walk will be great, if you're up to carrying that large parcel all the way."

117

Rob returned her smile. "At least it's light."

As they wove between pedestrians congesting the sidewalks, Charity was as fascinated with the bustle of yellow cabs as she had been the last time they were in New York. The hum of chatter mingled with the rumble of traffic filled the air.

Madison inhaled the scents of brewed java from a nearby coffee shop, nuts roasting at a nearby pretzel cart, and the smell of dough from a bagel shop they'd just passed.

Inside 30 Rockefeller Plaza, they took the elevator to the 65th floor. Madison's heart hammered in her throat as she and Charity followed Rob to The Gallery. Just beyond that lay the Rainbow Room where the gala event would take place tomorrow night.

As they stepped inside The Gallery, white plinths of varying heights and widths greeted them. Workers milled about between the columns, frantically getting everything ready for the arty event.

Madison gasped. "Wow!" She really shouldn't have been surprised that everything looked so elegant, even though none of the artworks had arrived yet. They were inside 30 Rockefeller Plaza, a place of timeless opulence.

Her pulse raced. She was about to meet Ellie Sanders…in the living flesh.

Rob pointed to the structures with his free hand. "There are twelve vertical rows of four spanning the length of the room with a single plinth on either end positioned in the center of the four horizontal rows."

Charity focused her gaze on Rob. "Why are some higher than me, while others would barely reach my knees?"

"There are artworks in various mediums and sizes that will be exhibited tomorrow," Rob explained. "That's why some are wider than others, some are square, and others are rectangular. Soon there'll be sculptures, wood carvings, and glassworks on display on those lower stands. The taller, rectangular ones will house paintings like your mother's."

"You mean mine?" Charity poked her index finger against her chest.

Rob shot Madison a puzzled look.

Patting his shoulder, Madison chuckled. "Don't worry, Rob. I *am* the artist. I recently painted the portrait as a sixteenth birthday gift for Charity. So, while she's the official owner, I am the artist. And of course, I do have her permission for this piece to be in the contest. You can ask her if you don't believe me."

"You just about gave me a heart attack." Rob heaved a relieved sigh. "There are rumors that *Girl in a Field* is tipped as one of the favorites to win, so I'm relieved to hear that Charity has given her okay. How her cherished Kansas piece had to be pulled from the contest is something I would hate to have to explain to Ellie."

"Explain what to Ellie?"

The mature woman's voice caused Rob, Madison, and Charity to whirl around.

Madison stared, even though her mother had taught her it was rude to do so. The sixty-something legend of the art world looked very different in real life as opposed to the professional photographs Madison had seen in glossy art magazines, as well as the Ellie Sanders Gallery website and on some TV shows. More down to earth dressed in a pair of jeans with a blue button-up shirt over her white T-shirt, sans the jewelry she usually dripped with. On her feet she wore comfortable, beige, slip-on espadrilles. Her straight, long bob—now a platinum-blond—hung loosely around her shoulders, not tied up in one of those fancy French twists that were so iconic of the talented artist. She wore minimal makeup, and sported a pair of dark rimmed, geometric-shaped glasses. Yet, even dressed down, Ellie Sanders had an elegance about her.

Even though they'd never met before, there was something so familiar about the woman that Madison only noticed now seeing her in person. But she couldn't place what.

Ellie held out a hand. "Madison Peterson. I'm *so* pleased to meet you."

After shaking Madison's hand, she turned to Charity. "And you must be—"

"The *Girl in a Field*." Charity grinned. "But you can call me Charity."

"What a beautiful name. And you are just as pretty as that picture your mother painted. Dressed like that, all we need to do is have you stand on one of those low plinths and you'll win the judges' hearts for sure." Ellie pointed to the backpack slung over Charity's shoulders. "But first, we'd need to relieve you of that. It's definitely not in the original."

Charity gave a nervous laugh.

Leaning closer, Ellie examined Charity's face. "You have your father's eyes."

Madison started at Ellie's observation. *What?* "You've met my husband?" Brody had never mentioned it before.

Ellie gave a light shrug. "Well, she doesn't have *your* eyes, Madison dear. You know that I'm all about the perfect shade of color, so even though your eyes are also blue, they're so much darker than Charity's. The natural assumption then is that she must have her fathers' eyes."

Oh, right.

Ellie's own light blue gaze sparkled with excitement as she turned to Rob and reached for the precious cargo that he'd rested on the glossy floor. "Is that it?"

Rob handed the package to Ellie. "Maddie says it is. I'm taking her word for it."

Ellie turned to Madison. "Do you mind if we unwrap it now? Don't worry, it'll be perfectly safe—the place where it will hang is ready and waiting. Soon the other artists will be arriving with their entries as well. And there will be 24-hour security."

Madison's heart beat faster. "Of course. Be my guest."

Laying the box on the floor, Ellie opened it. With Rob's help, she pulled the bubble wrapped canvas out. Pieces of scrunched up wadding that filled the gaps to ensure the painting didn't move, fell to the floor. Ellie loosened the masking tape securing the wrapping then freed the canvas from its plastic shroud. Lastly, she removed the cardboard Madison had used to cover the artwork in order to reduce the amount of static between the bubble wrap and the painting.

"Oh my..." Ellie's blue eyes widened. "This is even more incredible than I'd imagined. The technique is amazing, Madison. You're very talented." She pushed to her feet and propped the canvas against a nearby plinth to admire it further.

Madison couldn't stop a grin from spreading across her face. "Thank you, Ms. Sanders. That means a lot to me."

"Please, call me Ellie. Come." Ellie lifted the artwork and strode to the plinth standing on its own in front of the first row of four white columns. She hung the canvas on the hook that had been strategically placed at exactly the right height. It was as if the plinth had been made for Madison's painting. She stepped back to better examine the piece.

"I absolutely love the way you've captured the wheat waving in the breeze like an ocean of gold—Charity's hair at one with the sheaves." A soft sigh escaped Ellie's lips. "It reminds me of when I was that age, frolicking through the Kansas wheat fields. Young and in love..." Her voice trailed off so that Madison could barely make out her words. There seemed to be a sadness in her voice, and Madison couldn't help wondering if some Kansas boy had broken Ellie's heart.

Charity elbowed Madison and whispered, "Can you believe it, Mom. Your artwork will be the first thing anyone attending this exhibition and ceremony will see. What an honor to be placed there."

"Well, it's entirely possible that Ellie has just hung the painting there to get a better look at the piece," Madison whispered back.

Rob cleared his throat, drawing their attention. He motioned with his finger for Madison and Charity to follow him.

He stopped on the opposite side of the plinth where Madison's painting currently hung and pointed.

Madison glanced up and her hand flew to her mouth. "A–are you serious?" A canvas print of her face, the size of a sheet of writing paper, hung there. Beneath it, a smaller canvas with her name printed on it and 'Kansas' in bold letters beneath.

Madison stepped away to the first row of four plinths to check the backs of the columns. Each had the same two canvases hanging on them with various artists' faces, names, and the state they represented.

She felt so incredibly blessed. What had she done to deserve such a favorable placing? Nobody could miss her piece.

"Did you have something to do with this, Charity?" she asked her daughter. "Shoot a few prayers to heaven lately?"

Charity smiled. "Well, not specific prayers, but I do always pray for God's blessings on your life and Dad's. This is, no doubt, a result of those prayers, Mom. God is so good."

It seemed He was. How had she not discovered that yet?

Sadness shadowed her joyous moment. If only Brody were here to see this. She'd love to call him and tell him. Maybe she'd try to later tonight.

After another night of Chinese takeout, Brody settled himself on the couch to watch some of his favorite sitcoms. Maybe the humor of the shows would brighten his week, although nothing he'd watched since Monday night had managed to do so yet. Eating the same food every night, watching TV on your own… Well, it just wasn't any fun. It was lonely.

Of course, he was quite capable of cooking his own dinners, and he loved being creative in the kitchen, but what was the point without Madison by his side?

He flipped through the channels, nothing enticing him to watch.

Once Madison returned to Cottonwood Falls, could he go through with his threat for her not to come back if she went to New York? Maybe she'd decide to stay in New York with her parents? What if she kept his daughter there?

He should have followed her and demanded that Charity return to Cottonwood Falls with him.

On the couch beside him, his cell phone rang, breaking the silence that had clung to the walls of the house every night. He lifted it and glanced at the screen.

Madison.

Much as he wanted to hear her voice, he had nothing to say to her. She'd made her choice. Clearly she wasn't as devoted to him or their marriage vows as he'd thought.

He answered the call, then hung up without uttering a word, preventing Madison from even leaving a voicemail.

A few minutes later, the ringing started for the second time. Brody glanced at the screen once more.

Charity.

Probably Madison using their daughter's phone in an attempt to trick him into taking her call. Well, he wouldn't be caught for the fool.

This time he let the call go to voicemail.

A few minutes later, the phone rang for a third time. Brody snatched the phone and sprang to his feet, answering the call without looking. "Stop calling me. I *don't* want to talk to you."

"Whoa, Brody… It's me, Faith. And I haven't called you in at least three weeks."

Great! Now his sister would question him about who had pressed his buttons.

"Brody, what's going on? Who don't you want to talk to?"

Just as he thought.

Brody huffed and flopped onto the couch. He leaned his head into the backrest cushions and gazed up at the ceiling. "It's nothing."

"Hey, it's me you're talking to, remember?" Faith's voice soothed. "You know you can talk to me anytime, about anything. I won't judge you or preach to you. You'll get sound advice if you confide in me—you know that."

Brody sank lower in the couch, stretching his legs out. Faith would find out sooner or later anyway. And hadn't she and Charles gone through a really rough patch two years ago?—so rough that his sister had driven through the night with her son from Colorado to Kansas. And yet, look at them now—you couldn't find a more devoted and in love couple than Faith and Charles.

Yes, it *had* taken a serious car accident to make them realize that they still loved each other and wanted their marriage to work.

What will it take for you, Brody?

"Excuse me?" How had Faith known what he was thinking?

"Um, I didn't say anything," Faith said. "I'm still this side of the line, patiently waiting for you to tell me what's wrong."

Well if his sister hadn't said anything, who had, because he'd heard those words as clearly as if someone had spoken them in his ear?

Faith claimed that God used her accident to bring them back together again. Was it possible for Him to save his marriage too? Only if He saved Brody Peterson first—of that Brody was certain—and most days, he felt so unworthy of being saved.

Maybe he should just start by talking to his sister. He didn't have to delve into his deep, dark secrets.

Brody sucked in a deep breath and exhaled. "It's Madison. She's in New York with Charity. I'm afraid that I told her if she went, to never come back."

CHAPTER FOURTEEN

"MOM, you look incredible tonight. I wish Dad could see you."

Madison twisted in front of the cheval mirror, standing in a corner by the window of her hotel room, to get a good look at herself. She had chosen well with this embroidered, cap sleeve evening dress. And she adored the mauve color with nude underlay—gave the long figure-hugging gown a vintage feel.

She tucked a strand of hair, fallen out of the messy side bun, behind her ear and exhaled. Her heart ached not having Brody beside her tonight, looking dashingly handsome in a tuxedo, that cute ponytail of his hugging his collar like some dashing Renaissance artist.

Trying her best to ignore the heartache, she turned to Charity. "And you look simply lovely. Are you sure you don't mind wearing your birthday dress again? We really could've gone out shopping this morning for something new."

Charity rolled her eyes and flicked her long, strawberry-blond locks over her shoulder. "And put me through that misery all over again? Thanks, but no thanks, Mom. Once was enough. This dress is just fine."

Madison laughed. "Oh honey, but one day soon you're going to wake up to the pleasures of fashion. Then I won't be able to keep you out of Emporia's dress shops."

"We should go, Mom. We don't want to be late."

"Yes. And I do want to check out the competition before the awards ceremony and the dinner starts." Madison dabbed some of her favorite evening perfume on her pulse points, the exotic oriental notes reminding her so much of Brody. This was one of his favorite make up gifts.

She swallowed hard then grabbed her purse and headed for the door.

What an incredible feeling it was to walk into The Gallery, adorned with fifty artworks, and see her painting first. The place was alive with women in swishing ball gowns—some sequined from top to bottom, sparkling brightly beneath the lights—and well-groomed, tuxedo-clad men. The buzz of chatter threatened to drown out the jazz music playing in the background.

Three hundred artists and patrons of the arts had turned up for this auspicious event. Hopefully the place was full enough to be able to avoid her parents for the night. Madison wasn't in the mood for another of her mother's "Brody should be here by your side" speeches.

Soon everyone filtered through to the Rainbow Room, backdropped by twinkling city lights and decorated with chandeliers, candles, and huge arrangements of white flowers. Up on the stage, a band played. How she loved the smooth, romantic sound of a saxophone.

Madison sat down at her table near the stage, feeling a little less confident about taking the win. All the finalists' pieces were so creative. There was more than a handful of exceptional artworks. What a hard time the judges must've had choosing.

Charity sat in the seat on Madison's right.

Madison greeted the rest of the artists and their partners seated around the table. The two seats beside Charity were yet to be occupied. She cast her gaze around the room, relieved to see both Ellie and Rob seated at tables on the opposite side of the large, revolving dancefloor. The last thing she wanted was to be seen as the contestant who got way too much favor from the organizers. For a moment she lost herself in the darker compass rose image on the wooden surface. It reminded Madison of an ancient treasure map.

Ellie had told her earlier that the winning artwork would be showcased later on that pivotal point of the dancefloor.

The young man in his mid-twenties seated beside Madison leaned forward. "Aren't you the girl in the field?" Ignoring Madison, he directed his question past her to Charity.

Eyes lighting with interest, Charity nodded. Was that a blush tinting her daughter's cheeks? So she'd started to notice boys... Madison would need to make sure that the boy, or rather the man next to her, didn't take too much notice of her daughter. She recognized him from his photograph at the back of one of the plinths—a talented abstract artist from Louisiana—although she couldn't recall his name. She knew these arty types—far too much passion for their own good, and more often than not, the canvas wasn't a sufficient outlet for all those intense feelings. Probably half the reason she and Brody had married when she was so young. Well, she'd make certain that didn't happen to their daughter. The Kansas field was one this guy sitting beside her was *not* going to play in.

She turned to him. "Yes, she is. I recently painted that portrait of *my* daughter for her *sixteenth* birthday."

The guy shrank back, raising his brows. "Sixteen? Wow. I would've figured her for at least eighteen. She looks way more grown up than in the portrait. Great piece though. And great placement in the exhibition. They say that first impressions last."

Tongue in cheek, Madison replied, "Yes they do." Hopefully he'd realize he hadn't created a very good first impression on Madison at all. Humph, hitting on her daughter like that. He could channel all of that interest and admiration into the *Girl in a Field*. *Her* girl in the field...definitely not.

Madison smiled at the elderly woman who had claimed the chair beside Charity. She reached out and touched the woman's arm. "Georgia...right?"

"My name or my state?" The woman laughed. "Oh, I've gotten so much mileage out of that one tonight." She held out a hand to Madison. "I'm Georgia from Montana."

Madison smiled back at her. "We're literally neighbors...give or take two states. "Madison, from—"

"Kansas. *Girl in a Field*. Everyone is raving about that portrait. The innocence of youth shining through every brushstroke is incredible. You have such talent."

"Thank you. And so do you. I loved your rendition of the dancing Chippewa Cree. The expressions on those native Indians' faces, the bright colors of the feathers...so realistic. An amazing piece and so worthy of being here." In fact, that was one of the pieces Madison was worried about. Definitely a strong contender to win.

But none of that mattered now as Madison, Charity, and Georgia struck up a conversation. And a friendship.

They talked all the way through the three courses of dinner until Rob's microphoned voice drew their attention to the stage as he introduced the panel of seven judges—four men, three women— one of whom was Ellie Sanders.

Madison whispered to Georgia, "I have to know... Does he call you Georgie?"

Georgia chuckled and nodded her silvery head. "How did you know?"

Madison placed a hand on her chest. "Because I'm Maddie."

Looking oh-so-elegant in her long, sleeveless, sheath dress—the black a timeless classic, the beads giving the gown an extra touch of class—Ellie stepped up to the microphone. She smoothed a hand over her French twist. This was the Ellie Sanders the world knew.

"Thank you very much for the introductions, Robert. I trust everyone is having a good time tonight?" Her gaze roamed the room as cheers and whistles rose.

Ellie's smile grew wider. "That's wonderful. I know you've all been anxiously awaiting this moment, so without further ado, I'd like to announce the finalists and winner of the Art USA contest chosen by my esteemed colleagues and myself."

Ellie opened the envelope handed to her by Rob. She ripped open the back and pulled out a postcard-sized paper. "In third place is…"

The band gave a drumroll.

"Cole Johnson with his bronze sculpture, 'Golden Dreams'." Ellie put her hands together. "Let's hear it for our golden boy from the Golden State, California."

Madison had loved that piece. Made her want to just stretch right out beside the life-size bronzed beach babe lying on a towel.

A man around Brody's age, with his same build and artist's ponytail, rushed onto the stage to receive his trophy and winner's check from Ellie for ten thousand dollars. Cole Johnson raised the trophy above his head before shaking the hands of the other judges. He took his place beside them.

"A worthy win, don't you think?" Ellie turned to receive the second envelope from Rob and opened it.

"Taking second place and twenty thousand dollars in prize money, all the way from Big Sky Country…"

The drums rolled once more.

Beside Charity, Georgia's breath hitched and her hand flew to her mouth.

"Georgia Bell with her incredible palette knife oil painting on canvas of the dancing Chippewa Cree titled 'Pow-Wow'. So deserving of this place. And what a pow-wow Georgia gave us with those bright feathers—so real, you wanted to reach out and touch them, right?"

Georgia still sat glued to her seat, frozen with shock.

Madison leaned past Charity and shook Georgia's shoulder lightly. "That's you friend. Get on up there before they give that place to someone else."

Georgia nodded. "Yes, yes." She rose and hurried to the stage, shouting and waving her hands. "I'm coming. I'm coming."

Laughter rose around the banqueting hall.

Georgia was such a honey, and Madison couldn't be happier for her. But if Madison didn't take that first place, she would've wanted Georgia to have won the coveted prize. So in that sense, a twinge of disappointment mingled with her excitement.

Georgia repeated Cole's victory round then went to stand beside him.

Madison's heart thumped so hard in her chest now, she was certain those sitting close-by could hear it too. Then again, their hearts were probably also pounding, as were the hearts of all the other contestants.

Ellie opened the final envelope and clutched it to her chest with a sigh. "Oh, this one is so close to my heart, and while the judges' decision on the first place was unanimous, I want you all to know that I had no sway or influence over my esteemed peers."

Someone in the audience shouted out "Texas! The lone star!"

Ellie's mouth curved in a smile. "It gives me the greatest pleasure to award the grand prize to Madison Peterson from my home state for her fine art oil painting on canvas, *Girl in a Field*, along with fifty thousand dollars in prize money, *plus* an exclusive exhibition of the artist's work at the Ellie Sanders Gallery." She stretched out her arm, beckoning to Madison.

Charity shrieked, and somewhere in the room, Madison heard her father's voice boom, "That's my girl!"

This was a dream come true.

But it could also be the beginning of her worst nightmare.

Dear Jesus

Much as I had wanted to, I didn't get to write to You last night. Grandma and Grandpa, as well as Ellie Sanders and Rob, insisted that Mom and I stay and celebrate. It was a lot of fun, but we were both so exhausted by the time we got back to the hotel. What an exciting night. I'm just sad that my dad missed it.

I'm writing a quick note as I need to get up and get dressed for breakfast soon. Liam is picking up Mom and me at ten. I wish we weren't staying one more night with my grandparents. I just want to go home. I miss my dad. And I miss my dog. At least we'll be home tomorrow night.

If only Dad had taken Mom's calls, or mine for that matter...maybe then I wouldn't be feeling quite as homesick. Or worried. I don't know how my father will react when we get home. He hasn't answered any calls, or responded to our texts or voicemails. If his silent treatment is anything to go on...

Well, You've told me not to worry—about anything—so I'm just going to take a deep breath and leave this messy situation in Your hands, because I know that no matter how bad something might be, You will work everything for good just because I love You and am called by You. That's what Your word says.

So I choose to trust You. In everything.

Please change my father's mind about Mom having entered, and won, the contest. Please let him be as happy and as proud of her as I am. You have given my mother so much talent, and the world should get to see and enjoy it more.

Help my dad to agree to come to New York for Ellie Sanders's exhibition, which might not even happen at this stage as most of Mom's work is tied up in the gallery. I know she's concerned about that, so I pray that You will work this out...for all our sakes.

With love
Charity
(Daughter of the King)

CHAPTER FIFTEEN

SEATED ON the plane at Newark airport bound for Kansas City, Madison's mind mulled over the events of the day before. Both she and Charity had tried to steer the conversations over lunch and dinner to the gala event and her win. However, during dessert last night, Mother had finally come right out and asked what Charity had meant on Friday about Brody kicking them out. Father was shocked at the question and demanded to know what was going on. Madison stood her ground, telling her parents that her marriage was none of their concern. Or their business.

"Well, if there's any truth in what Charity said, know that you both will always have a home here," Father had reassured her.

Humph, as if she would be able to live under the same roof as her mother for an indefinite period of time.

Madison turned to Charity, seated at the window. "Honey, I'm going to get some shut-eye for the next three hours. I'm still pretty tired from Saturday, and we have at least a two-hour drive back home once we land. It'll be seven before we get back to Cottonwood Falls, maybe even heading toward eight o'clock, depending on the traffic.

Charity's eyes brightened. "I can help with the driving, Mom."

"Yes, of course, you can. I keep forgetting that you're a licensed driver now. It'll be good practice for you as well. As long as the road back home isn't too busy."

Madison closed her eyes, and by the time she opened them again, the flight attendant was calling for passengers to fasten their seatbelts as the plane was commencing its descent. She hadn't realized just *how* exhausted she had been. But the past week had been emotionally taxing, bearing the silent treatment from Brody. How she would've loved to have had him share all the excitement with her.

Instead…

She blew out a sigh and checked her seatbelt, realizing that she'd never unbuckled it since taking off in New York.

Once Madison and Charity had retrieved their luggage from the baggage carousel, they headed to the long-term parking where Madison had parked her car. At least they didn't have the painting to contend with as well. Ellie Sanders had already taken that to exhibit in her gallery. In a month's time they would return to New York for the opening of the Madison Peterson exhibition at the Ellie Sanders Gallery. Hopefully, Brody would come to terms with everything long before then and accompany her. School would have just started. Well, Charity would need to miss the Friday and Monday because Madison didn't want to do this without her daughter experiencing it too. And who knows, maybe it would spark that creativity in Charity that Madison knew existed deep down inside of her. With her and Brody's genes, how could her daughter not also have incredible talent?

Their luggage stowed in the car, Madison turned to Charity. "Honey, let me drive us out of the city. Once we're on the I-35, I'll find a rest stop to pull over and we can switch seats. Okay?"

"Perfect, Mom. I'd never be able to drive in all this traffic. I'm quite happy to wait until there are only a few cars on the road."

They'd driven for three-quarters of an hour before Madison veered right on Exit 210 near Gardner. She pulled in at the rest stop and Charity took over the driving.

Just as well Madison had slept on the plane. She didn't realize she'd be this nervous having her daughter drive on the big, open roads for the first time. Not that Charity was a bad driver by any means—Madison was just an over-cautious mom.

The closer they got to Cottonwood Falls, the harder Madison's heart pounded.

Charity shot her a glance. "You're very quiet. Are you scared?"

Madison nodded. She swallowed hard, fighting her tears. She couldn't shake the premonition that things would not go well.

"Don't worry, Mom. Jesus tells us not to. Remember that no matter what happens, He's in control."

Oh, if only she had the same faith as her daughter.

Maybe if her parents had let her go to Sunday school and church…

As Charity drove up their driveway, she pressed the garage remote. The door slowly rolled up, and Madison's lungs constricted, refusing to give air.

Brody's SUV was in the garage. He was home. Any minute now, there'd be a confrontation. Why hadn't she dropped Charity at Sandy's house instead so that her daughter could be spared this showdown? But it was too late now. Besides, Charity had missed her dad and was excited she'd be seeing him soon.

They entered the kitchen through the garage door, dragging their luggage behind them.

Brody stood in front of the oven, an apron tied around his waist like always when he was cooking. A meaty aroma permeated the air, assailing Madison's senses. Dinner smelled so good.

Hearing them, Brody pivoted.

And wow, her husband looked so good, despite time having

136

marched on from the usual five-o-clock shadow that graced his jawline. Her stomach gave a little growl; her heart a thump. She was hungry—and for more than just the food.

"Dad, I've missed you." Charity rushed toward him, wrapping her arms around his neck. She pinched the longer stubble on his cheek between her fingers and gave a tug. "And this? Your electric razor not working?"

Ignoring Madison, Brody shrugged. He wouldn't even look her way. "No time to shave. It's been a busy week running the business *and* house on my own." A caustic tone coated his words.

"Dinner will be ready in about thirty minutes. Run upstairs and take a bath, or unpack, or something. Your mother and I need to be alone to talk."

Madison's pulse raced so fast, she felt dizzy and positively ill as Charity walked away, carry-on bag in one hand, dragging the larger suitcase behind her with the other as she left Madison to face the Brody music alone.

Lord, help me, she prayed, not knowing if God would answer. She'd never paid Him much attention before. Would the Almighty take any notice of her crisis prayers?

Needing more time to brace herself for what was about to come, Madison spoke to Brody's back. "D–do you mind if I shower first? I–it's been a long day. I'll be quick, I promise."

"Whatever. I'll be here."

Madison clutched her bags and started to walk away.

"Leave those there." Brody's sharp, brash tone knifed Madison's heart. "I'll bring them."

Well, things couldn't be that bad. At least he hadn't forgotten how to be a gentleman and help a lady.

Madison raced upstairs, eager to keep her promise not to take long, totally unprepared for the sight before her as she walked into their bedroom. Her body began to tremble. Two large suitcases stood in front of her dresser.

What? Was Brody leaving her?

Or—

She turned and slammed into the virile chest she had loved to caress for over seventeen years. Now it was hard and uninviting. She looked up at her husband, tears threatening to spill over. "Brody…w–what is this?"

"Your things. Or at least enough to tide you over until you can get the rest. I didn't want Charity to see. I'll take your suitcases to the car."

"What? W–why are you doing this?" She thought by now he would have seen the error of his ways. But it seemed the only mistakes he saw, were hers.

"I told you, Madison… I warned you that if you went to New York, not to come back to me. You made your choice." His blue eyes, usually warm with ardor, were as cold as their icy color.

"For the betterment of us, of our business," Madison argued. "That's why I went."

"We didn't need betterment. But you made your choice, Madison. And it wasn't me. I want you to go. Now!" Brody pushed past her and wrapped his fingers around the suitcase handles. He wheeled the bags toward the door.

Madison grabbed his shirt's sleeve. "Brody, don't do this. Not over something I did for the two of us."

He spun around. "You're just like her! Walking out on me, putting your career before your family. Finding excuses to pursue your own dreams!"

What was he talking about?

"Like who?"

He stared at her, nostrils flaring, breathing hard.

"Like who, Brody?" Madison asked again.

He shook his head. "It doesn't matter. Just leave. Now!"

Hands still shaking from anger at Madison and the stark realization of what he'd just done, Brody set a bowl of herbed potato salad down in the middle of the kitchen table. He'd seen Madison's text about what time they anticipated being home, so he was able to prepare dinner for Charity, but he'd resolved that Madison would be gone before they sat down to eat.

Charity blew into the kitchen, still clothed in the jeans and T-shirt she'd returned home in, and sank into her seat at the table. She must have used the time in her room to unpack. He hadn't thought she'd opt for a bath this early. She set her cell phone down on the table, her gaze oscillating between the two plates, and her smile faded. "Why are there only two places set? Where's, Mom?"

"She won't be joining us for dinner tonight." *Or any other night.* The thought pained him. But it couldn't be helped. He'd rather be the one to do the discarding, than be the one discarded soon enough.

Again.

History repeating itself.

The pain of the bitter memory dug deep, hurting just as much as it had so long ago.

He pulled the rack of ribs from the oven and set them down on the counter. He cut the rack in two, one side slightly bigger than the other, then dished the smaller rack onto Charity's plate.

"Is she feeling unwell? Lying down upstairs?" His daughter's bright blue eyes held his, searching for answers.

"She's…" What did he say? I kicked your mother out into the night? No child would take that news well. What had he been thinking?

But what was done, was done.

Settled in his chair, Brody lifted his knife and fork, even though the events of the night had left his appetite waning. "Let's eat. We'll talk later, okay, sweetheart?"

Charity cleared her throat. "Um, can I say grace for us, Dad?"

Knife hovering above the rack, ready to slice, Brody paused. He nodded. "Of course."

Charity closed her eyes, and Brody imitated her.

"Dear Lord Jesus, thank You for bringing Mom and me back safely. Thank You for blessing her so. Thank You for her talent. If she's ill, I pray that You'll help her to feel well again, and if she's just tired, give her sweet sleep. Will you bless this food to us, Lord Jesus, and bless the hands that prepared it." She gave a soft chuckle. "That's my dad's hands."

Brody shifted uncomfortably in his seat. He had just told his daughter's mother to leave, and here Charity was praying for his hands to be blessed. The same hands that had carried Madison's suitcases to her car and flung them inside in white hot anger. Would she still pray the same blessing once she knew?

"In Your mighty name I pray. Amen," his sweet girl concluded.

Charity was about a third of the way through her meal when she set her knife and fork down. "I'm going to run upstairs and see if Mom wants something to eat."

"Charity… Don't."

"Why?" Her gaze questioned as she started to ease out of her chair.

He wasn't going to dodge this explanation tonight. "B–because your mother isn't upstairs."

Palms on the table as she half stood, Charity froze. "Where is she then?"

"I–I don't know." Although he suspected she'd go to Sandy's house. Then again, it was entirely possible for her to check into a hotel as well.

Lines rippled across her brow as what was left of her smile

vanished. Her voice cracked, "W–what do you mean, you don't know, Dad?"

Brody expelled the air from his lungs, then breathed in deeply. "Did your mother tell you that when she informed me about entering the contest, I warned her? I told her that if she went to New York, she wasn't to come back to me."

His knife and fork clunked against the porcelain plate as he dropped the utensils and stared his daughter down. "She made her choice, Charity—don't make me the bad guy here."

"Why Dad? Why are you so threatened by her entering? Did you submit an entry to the contest and now you're annoyed that *you* weren't the one who finaled? Why are you so jealous of Mom?" Charity wailed as she pushed to her full height, looking down on Brody.

He shook his head. "I didn't enter the contest, Charity. And I'm not jealous of your mother. T–there are things you don't know, don't understand. If I could tell you, you would realize why the stance I've taken is for the good of this family."

Charity's eyes widened as she crossed her arms, jutting out one jean-clad hip. "For the good of this family? Wha—? Dad, you just broke up this family!"

She turned and ran from the kitchen leaving Brody to stew on her words.

Dear Jesus

My heart is broken. My faith is fragile. Even so, I will choose to trust You, that You will remain true to Your Word that all things work together for good to them that love God, to them who are called according to his purpose.

I don't think I can cry any more tears, but I thank You that not one is wasted, that you see each one I shed. They're so precious to You that You keep them stored in a bottle; You write each one down so they're not forgotten.

Forgive me, Lord, for breaking Your command to obey my mother and father. I'm sorry, but I just couldn't open the door when my dad knocked on it tonight. I couldn't talk to him. Not now. Even though he said he was sorry.

I wish I hadn't left my phone on the kitchen table. How I would've loved to call Mom to hear if she is all right. I'm sure she'll be at Aunt Sandy's, so I know she's in good hands.

Though maybe it's better if I don't talk to my parents right now. I need to take a step back—in fact a lot of steps back. I need to be far away from this situation because I'm so confused right now. I have no idea what happened here tonight. I don't understand my father's reasoning, or why You have allowed things to come to this. All I know is that I can't stand being in this house with its turmoil any longer. I know what I need to do—soon as Dad has left for work in the morning—and I pray that You will help me and keep me safe. If I don't do this immediately, I never will, and things will probably go on as they always have—nothing will change, and I could bear that even less.

Thankfully I never unpacked my bags earlier, choosing to spend the time with You instead. Thank you for supplying what I will need in all that money I got for my birthday from my grandpa and grandmother.

If my parents can't reconcile, they'll expect me to choose between them.

I can't.

And I won't.

I know You'll understand my actions.

All my love

Your beloved child
Charity

CHAPTER SIXTEEN

"YOU LOOK awful." Sandy set a mug of coffee down on her kitchen table in front of Madison.

Wrapping her hands around the smooth, warm surface, Madison gazed up at her friend through swollen eyes, unable to muster a smile. "Thanks. You certainly know how to cheer a girl up."

Sandy grinned. "I hope you're talking about the coffee. And you're welcome."

Madison shook her head.

"As for your appearance…just the honest truth. There's no hiding that." Sandy slid onto the seat next to Madison, reached for her hand and squeezed. "But you still look beautiful in your awfulness, if there's such a thing."

She stared at Madison as if examining her red-rimmed eyes, scrutinizing every line Madison felt had materialized on her face this morning. "I do wish you'd slept late though."

Madison sighed. "I couldn't. In fact, I don't think I slept much at all last night."

Sandy sipped her coffee, her brows rising above the mug's rim. She swallowed the liquid. "So, we can't blame those eyes on tears alone?"

Elbows to the table, Madison rested her brow against her palms and shook her head. "Everything is such a mess. My marriage. My future—I don't even know to what extent my daughter will be a part of that. My career. And now the exhibition too." She leaned back and stared at Sandy. "If Brody refuses to let me have my artworks back, I'll have nothing to send Ellie and not enough time to paint sufficient new pieces. I only have a handful in the studio, and for all I know, Brody might've already changed the house locks. I might not be able to retrieve my canvases, easels, paints, and brushes."

"He wouldn't be *that* cruel, would he?" Her soft gaze sympathetic to Madison's quandary, Sandy twirled the spoon that lay on the table in front of her.

Madison shrugged, closing her eyes for a brief moment to gather her thoughts. "Who knows what Brody is capable of at the moment? It's as if I don't know him. I'm so puzzled by his behavior and the things he has said and done. Do you think he was perhaps in a serious relationship before I met him—maybe even engaged—and had his heart broken by some other woman? It's the only explanation I can think of for him accusing me of being 'just like *her*'. Whoever this woman was in his life, she must've put her career before him. Now he's terrified I'll do the same."

Sandy stopped twirling the spoon for which Madison was thankful. It was beginning to grate on her frayed nerves. She smiled. "Which you would never do, Mads. I know you. You're so committed to Brody, so in love with him—despite your frequent blow ups. It's hard to comprehend why he can't see that."

Madison sighed again. "What I did by entering Art USA and then going to New York, I did for us, for our business. Definitely not for any self-gain—although there were times I doubted my motivation. I–I thought this would be good for us, but I guess I was wrong."

Baxter bounded into the kitchen, excited to see Madison again. He'd reacted the same way last night when she'd arrived on Sandy's doorstep. His tail thwacked against the legs of Madison's chair, then Sandy's.

Madison reached down and ruffled his coat. "Hey, boy. You hungry? You want some food?"

Melinda rushed into the kitchen, relief flooding her face. "Oh good, there you are. Bad dog!" She scooped Baxter up into her arms. "He's so fast when he slips through the slightest gap to escape a room."

"Tell me about it. And Charity." Tears welled again in Madison's eyes at the thought of her daughter, alone at home. Unless Brody had taken the day off to spend with her. If only Charity would answer her calls she could know if it was safe to pop home for a short while. Maybe Brody had confiscated her phone.

"Mom, I'm walking down to Charity with Baxter. She's dy— I'm sure she's dying to get him back." Melinda laughed. "And I can surely do with a break from him."

Melinda's gaze shot to Madison. "Oh, don't get me wrong, Aunt Mads. I've loved every minute of having him, but he can be quite a handful."

Didn't she know that so well?

Madison jumped at an excuse to go home. "I can drive you there."

Melinda shook her head. "That's not at all necessary. Really. Baxter needs the exercise, as do I. And I think under the circumstances, Charity just needs a friend around to cheer her up. No parents—again, no offense, Aunt Mads—just me and her for the day. Okay?"

Madison nodded. "I get it. I'm like that too. When I'm miserable, all I want is my best friend." She glanced at Sandy and turned her bottom lip down.

Sandy leaned closer and drew her into a hug. "Oh my friend. This, too, will pass."

"I'll be on my way then." Melinda waved and turned.

"Not so fast, young lady," Sandy barked. "What about breakfast?"

Melinda shrugged. "I'll get something to eat at Aunt Mads's house. She always has yummy food in the fridge."

"Yes, she does," Sandy said. "But remember that she's been away for a week."

The teenager flashed her mother a cheeky smile. "I'll take my chances."

"W–will you give her my love?" Madison asked. "Tell her that I've been calling and texting. Ask her to call me. Please."

"I will. See you later." Melinda exited the kitchen, Baxter quite happy to be in her arms.

Brody didn't bother to pull his SUV into the garage as he planned to treat Charity to supper. Whatever she was in the mood to eat. And if that was strawberry banana pancakes at Crepes, he'd drive all the way back to Emporia for her. Anything to keep his little girl happy. Especially now.

He had felt bad leaving her home alone all day, so he'd arranged to take tomorrow off. Yes, Wednesday's were Ava's half day off, but his assistant had jumped at the opportunity to be trusted with more responsibilities in the gallery, opting to take Thursday afternoon off instead, but only if Brody could spare her.

He did need to delegate more to Ava, especially now that Madison would no longer be an integral part of the business. Would she even be any part? He couldn't see how he could work with his wife any longer, given the circumstances. Besides,

Madison now had the endorsement of the great Ellie Sanders—why would she need Peterson Galleries to make a living? Not to mention the 50K she'd won. That would go some ways to setting up her own gallery or studio. Likely, she'd go home to Daddy, so he needn't worry that she wouldn't have a roof over her head.

Madison would be set, and she'd be well taken care of.

This is what she'd wanted. So this is what she got.

But one thing she wouldn't get—Charity. He would fight Madison with everything he possessed to keep custody of his daughter and continue to raise her in Cottonwood Falls. Many men were single fathers today. He had no doubt he could do it too.

He opened the front door and shouted, "Charity!"

Only a deathly quiet answered him.

She was probably in her room with her headphones on.

Brody bolted up the stairs, his pulse beating faster. Her bedroom door stood open, and he rushed inside.

Empty.

His gaze lowered, and he spotted the prayer journal Faith had given Charity for her birthday lying on the floor near her bed. He picked it up and set it down on the nightstand beside her bed.

Had she gone out? To find her mother maybe?

Brody took the stairs two at a time on his way down.

Standing at the open door between the kitchen and the garage, Brody stared at the emptiness that greeted him. She must've gone to Sandy's house.

He yanked his cell phone from his shirt pocket and tried Charity's phone. It rang several times before diverting to voicemail.

"Charity, honey, where are you? Call me."

Heaving a sigh, he dialed Madison's number for the first time in over a week.

Standing in front of the black, marble-topped island in the middle of Sandy's kitchen, Madison cut the freshly-peeled carrots into thick slices. She turned to Sandy. "I can't understand why I haven't been able to raise Charity on her phone since last night."

She lifted the board with the carrot slices and turned to the stove to drop the orange vegetables into the bright green Dutch oven beside Sandy's newly-added potatoes. The carrots sank into the dark, meaty sauce of her friend's famed All-American Beef Stew, laden with chunks of meat, onion, garlic, and spices.

"Brody *must've* confiscated it as punishment for going with me to New York," Madison said. "It's the only explanation I can give for Charity not answering or returning my calls."

"Maybe." Sandy covered the pot once again with the heavy lid.

Madison and Sandy worked well together in the kitchen.

Almost as well as she and Brody always had.

Her heart squeezed.

Sandy brushed her blond hair from her face then placed her hand on her hip, the dishtowel she'd used to move the hot lid dangling from her fingers. "If my daughter hadn't been in such a rush this morning and left her phone at home, you could've contacted Charity that way. Melinda should be home soon though. We can find out everything once she's back. Maybe Charity will even bring her home in her car? Then you can see your baby and ask her yourself."

Sinking onto a stool beside the island, Madison sighed. She lifted her wine glass and took a sip of the fruity white liquid Sandy had poured earlier. "I hope so."

The front door banged shut, drawing their attention.

Sandy's brows quirked. "Speaking of the devil…"

"Hi, Mom. Bye, Mom." Melinda's feet pounded up the stairs.

Sandy threw the dishtowel down and shouted, "Wait a minute... Where are you going young lady?"

"I'll be down shortly, Mom." Melinda's bedroom door slammed shut.

What on earth was her daughter's friend up to?

Madison resisted the urge to scurry up those stairs to ask the teen herself, but with dinner nearly ready, Melinda would be down soon enough. Then she could ask for explanations to her heart's content.

Madison's gaze shifted to where Sandy joined her on the opposite side of the high island.

A cell phone chimed and Sandy reached for the phone beside her. "It's yours." She handed the phone to Madison.

One glance at the caller ID and Madison's heart slammed into her ribs.

Brody?

"Hey," she answered in a soft voice, praying he was calling to reconcile.

"Is Charity there with you?" Still no warmth in her husband's voice. He still sounded just as angry with her as he'd been since she'd told him about the contest.

"No... I haven't seen or spoken with her today. Why?"

"She's not at home."

Unease washed over Madison. "S–she must be. Melinda was with her all day." Unless... "Listen, Melinda just walked in. Perhaps Charity dropped her off and she's headed back home as we speak. I'll run upstairs and check with her. I'll call you back."

"No!" Brody snapped, then his voice softened as he continued, "I'd rather hold, if you don't mind."

"All right..." Madison rose.

Sandy looked up, her frown questioning as she mouthed, *Is everything all right?*

Madison nodded. At least, she hoped everything was all right, that there was a simple explanation as to why Charity wasn't home.

The two friends raced upstairs to Melinda's bedroom door. Reaching it, Sandy knocked. "Melinda, can we come inside?"

A moment's silence ensued before Melinda responded, "Sure, Mom."

Sandy opened the door and swung it wide.

Madison stepped inside after her.

Melinda's head snapped toward them from where she sat cross-legged on her bed, phone discarded beside her.

"Melinda, sweetheart…" Madison neared the bed. "Did Charity bring you home in her car?"

Wide, innocent eyes—perhaps a little too innocent—stared back at Madison. The teenager shook her head. "No, Aunt Mads. I walked home. Oh, and I left Baxter with Charity. I hope that's okay, seeing as she's back."

"That's fine. So Charity was still at home when you left?" Madison pressed.

Melinda lowered her head and tucked her hands under her legs. She breathed in deeply and nodded.

What wasn't she telling them? Or was Madison merely imagining she was hiding something. Teens these days didn't like to make eye-contact with adults at the best of times—particularly if they thought they were in trouble over something.

"D–did she say if she was going somewhere?" Madison wasn't sure if she'd get an honest answer out of Melinda.

Melinda's pink lips pursed together and her brown bob swayed as she shook her head.

Madison exhaled. "All right."

She turned to go then paused. "Do you know why Charity didn't answer my calls or texts today?"

"Um…Mr. Peterson took her phone away from her last night."

She knew it. The louse.

Speaking of, she'd totally forgotten she'd muted the call and Brody was still on the phone.

"Please let me know if you hear from her."

"I will, Aunt Mads." Melinda shifted her gaze to her mother. "Is dinner ready yet, Mom? I'm starving, and it smells sooo good."

Sandy smiled. "Fifteen to twenty minutes. We'll see you downstairs after you've washed up."

Madison unmuted the call as she strode toward the staircase. "Brody? You still there?"

"Yes. A–any news from Melinda on Charity?" Concern clung to his words like wet paint to a palette.

"She claims Charity was still at home when she left. That couldn't have been more than a half hour ago. Maybe she went down to the store to get something for dinner. Or to see another friend."

"I don't like it, Madison. This isn't like her at all. I'm worried."

She didn't need him flipping out about something else now. "Brody. I'm sure she's fine. She's a good driver. Drove most of the way home yesterday from Kansas City. She's probably gone down to see Shana. Or Ethan. That's all."

"We should call them."

Sigh. Typical Brody to get all paranoid. Then again, it did seem as if Melinda wasn't being totally forthcoming. They'd probably find their daughter was visiting Ethan. Now that Madison realized her baby was starting to notice boys, it would make sense that Melinda would hide such information from her best friend's parents.

"Brody, give her another thirty minutes. If she's not home by six thirty, message me and I'll call Candice to ask Shana, and you can call Duncan to check with Ethan. All right?"

Brody huffed out an okay.

"Don't worry, honey. I'm sure she's fine," Madison soothed before she cut the call. By now she had followed Sandy all the way into the kitchen.

Her friend paused beside the stove and lifted the Dutch oven's lid. She stirred the bubbling liquid, shifting the meat and vegetables around.

"Hmm, looks good." Madison closed her eyes and inhaled deeply. "Smells even better."

Sandy set the lid back on the pot. "So where do you think Charity has disappeared to? Because I have a feeling that my daughter isn't telling us the whole truth."

"I get that feeling too. If she isn't, then I'd hazard a guess Charity is visiting a boy…probably Ethan. It's not surprising that my sweet girl would act out like this, even though it is out of character for her. This situation between me and Brody is hurting her, so I don't blame her really."

"For sure she's hurting, Mads." Sandy touched Madison's shoulder and gave it a light squeeze. "I'll see if I can get anything out of Melinda over dinner, okay?"

Madison shook her head. "Don't. I don't want to cause problems between you two. I'm sure Charity will be home soon. She may be upset, but she has a good head on her shoulders."

She rubbed her hands together and ran her tongue over her lips. "How much longer until we eat. I'm literally salivating for that stew of yours."

Sandy chuckled. "You sound just like Melinda. I think ten more minutes and the vegetables will be soft. Then I just need to thicken the sauce. So, thirteen minutes tops, I'd say. Why don't you set the table in the meantime?"

By six thirty, they'd finished eating and their dirty plates and silverware had been stacked in the dishwasher. Melinda quickly excused herself to take a shower. Madison and Sandy agreed that was just a ploy to avoid them, but what could they do?

Madison was busy wiping the granite island top when her phone buzzed with an incoming text. Her heart beat faster as she picked up the phone and read the message from her husband.

CHARITY STILL NOT HOME. I'M CALLING DUNCAN. PLEASE CONTACT CANDICE. I'LL LET YOU KNOW WHAT I HEAR.

Hand's trembling, she dialed Candice.

Her friend answered in her usual cheerful voice. "Madison, hi. So good to hear from you. It's been a while."

"Hi Candice. Sorry. I was out of town last week. Listen, I hate to cut to the chase, but is Charity perhaps visiting with Shana?"

"Charity? Noooo. We haven't seen her in at least two or three weeks. Is something wrong?"

Legs weakening, Madison slumped onto the nearest stool. "I… It's probably nothing, but we don't know where Charity is. She's been missing for the past hour and we can't get in touch with her."

"I'm sure she'll be home soon," Candice said. "Try not to fret."

An incoming call beeped in Madison's ear.

"I have to go."

"Please keep me posted." Candice cut the call.

"Any news?" Madison asked anxiously the moment she answered Brody's call.

"Nothing. They haven't seen or heard from Charity in at least two weeks. A–and you?"

"Same news from Candice."

"Babe, I'm really worried." Brody's voice broke and it sounded as if he might be crying. "This is my fault."

"Honey, just sit tight. I'll be there in five minutes."

CHAPTER SEVENTEEN

AT HOME, Madison pulled her Mini Cooper to a stop in the driveway.

Brody stood there waiting for her, still dressed in the suit pants and formal shirt he'd worn to work. Normally by this time, he'd changed into something more casual.

As soon as she stepped out of the car, he wrapped his arms around her.

She hugged him back, worried too. Already, she'd shot several prayers to heaven on the way over from Sandy's house, hoping that God would hear them.

Brody buried his head in her neck and sobbed. "What have we done? What have *I* done? If something happens to her, I–I'll never forgive myself."

Madison didn't want to entertain any of the possibilities of what could've happened to their daughter. Her mind churned over the alternatives, every one scarier than the last.

"We should go to the police and report her missing." Brody wiped his eyes as he sniffed. He wove his fingers between Madison's then led her inside.

"H–have you checked her bedroom? Noticed if anything is

missing?" There might be something that would give them some indication of where she could be.

"I haven't. Besides, I wouldn't know if anything was missing or out of place. Although…" He glanced toward the staircase. "I did find the prayer journal Faith recently bought her lying on the floor beside her bed. It seemed as if she'd dropped it there."

That didn't sound like something Charity would do. Baxter would find it and soon sink his teeth into its precious pages. That journal was almost as sacred to Charity as her Bible was.

"Let's check her room first." Madison started toward the staircase. "I'll soon know if anything isn't there."

Upstairs in their daughter's room, Madison scanned the closets and shelves. Hmm, none of the clothes she had packed for Charity for their New York trip were there.

She whirled around to face Brody. "Where's the suitcase Charity took to New York?"

Brody sank onto the edge of their daughter's bed. "I don't know. She took it upstairs with her last night when you were still here. Later, when Charity discovered that I'd told you to leave, she ran up to her room and locked herself inside. I haven't seen her since. I–I guess her suitcase should still be here, unless she unpacked it today and took it back to the garage. I can check."

Madison shook her head. "Don't bother. She hasn't unpacked. None of the clothes she took with her are in her closet. And I should know—I packed her bag."

"Maybe she emptied the suitcase and dumped the clothes in the laundry bin?"

"She wouldn't have. My mother was very particular that her maids washed and ironed our clothes every day. Charity still boasted that she had a suitcase bursting with clean clothes in case—" She clamped her teeth around her bottom lip. Brody didn't need to know what Charity had been thinking. He was feeling bad enough as it was.

He gazed up at her, a frown creasing his brow. "In case what, Madison?"

"N–nothing."

He rose and stood in front of her, taking her hands in his. "It's not nothing. I know you. In case what?"

Madison expelled the air from her lungs with a heavy sigh. "In case you kicked us out."

She wished she could have spared him the pained expression that resulted from her words.

"I'm sorry," he whispered."

Madison's eyes flitted around the room to see if Charity had left a note. Nothing. Her gaze came to rest on the bright red poppies of her daughter's prayer journal and she reached for the book. She eased down on the bed beside the pillow, one finger trailing the edge of a poppy. Dare she open and read what her daughter had written of late? Normally she'd respect Charity's privacy, but the circumstances were unusual, even dire. And they *could* find the answer within these pages to where Charity could be.

She gazed up at Brody and motioned for him to sit down beside her. This was something they needed to do together.

Brody's heart shattered as he read the entries in Charity's journal, starting from the final one she'd written last night. What had he and Madison done to their beautiful girl?

Correction. He was passing the buck again. How had *he* stirred up such havoc? Somehow, he'd hardened his heart and refused to see the pain he was causing both his wife and his daughter. Madison—the one he had sworn to cherish—his daughter, their precious gift from God.

Madison sobbed softly, turning back a page every time Brody

nodded that he was finished reading.

Words from the book containing his daughter's handwriting penetrated his mind as if some unearthly power made them rise from the cream-colored paper.

My heart is broken... Don't think I can cry any more tears... Couldn't open the door when my dad knocked... Better if I don't talk to my parents right now... A lot of steps back... Far away from this situation... Don't understand my father's reasoning... Can't stand being in this house with its turmoil... Know what I need to do... Soon as Dad has left for work in the morning...

Madison stopped and pointed to the words Brody had just read. "Does this mean she's possibly been gone for over eleven hours, not one?" Her eyes widened as realization dawned. "That would mean Melinda lied."

She started to rise. "She wasn't with Charity all day—she was covering for her. But she definitely had seen her because she returned without Baxter." She whipped her phone out of her pants' pocket. "I need to call Sandy."

Brody stopped her. "Honey, sit. Let's finish reading first—it's only a few entries, and it might give us some insight into where she could've gone."

Madison nodded and sank onto the mattress again. "You're right."

They continued reading where they'd left off. And the words continued to dance before his very eyes.

Nothing will change, and I could bear that even less... Never unpacked... Supplying what I will need... All that money from my grandpa and grandmother... Choose between them... I can't.... I won't... You'll understand my actions... My dad to agree to come to New York for Ellie Sanders's exhibition...

Over his dead body.

He exhaled a heavy sigh. Did it really matter anymore?

Wouldn't it be better for everyone concerned if he told them his deepest secret? Maybe if he did that, they could all move forward from there.

Together.

But how, when he'd carried this burden alone for so long?

Madison lifted the page to turn it, but Brody stopped her. Sidetracked with his thoughts, he hadn't quite finished the entry.

So worried that this could be the fight they don't recover from… Don't want to have divorced parents…

Brody turned the page this time to the very first entry.

Just one perfect day is all I wanted… Aunt Faith…she always knows how to make me feel better… Only You can paint a beautiful picture of their lives… Help me to forgive my parents again.

He needed to read more. Know more.

Brody leaned past Madison and opened the nightstand drawer. *Yes!* Charity's previous journal lay inside. He lifted it and immediately opened to the back. He read until he came to an entry, ten days before her birthday.

I wish every day at home could be filled with as much love and fun as tonight… Hate it when Mom and Dad argue… That's the reason I gave up painting… Irrational, jealous, possessive, unreasonable, and inflexible people…

That was how she saw them, why she no longer expressed herself artistically, except on these pages? He fingered the beautiful pen sketch beneath that journal entry, not nearly long enough to fill the page so she'd drawn a rose to fill the blank space. *They* were to blame?

His mind sped through their arguments, the tantrums, raised voices, heated words…

They'd been so busy sparring in stupid fights, they never realized their marriage was breaking. Could he and Madison ever fix things between them?

Not unless you let Me help you…

There was that voice again. Just like on the phone the other night with Faith.

Madison eased the journal from Brody's hands. Together with the new one she'd held, she set them down on the nightstand before twisting around to face him. "C–can I ask you something?"

Brody swallowed hard, unsure what question was headed his way. "Of course."

"Why did you confiscate Charity's phone? If you hadn't, we would be able to get in touch with her right now."

What was she talking about?

"I didn't take away her phone. She left it on the kitchen table last night. It was still there when I left this morning. Come to think of it, I didn't notice it there tonight."

Madison groaned. "Melinda… She *was* lying to me. She said you'd taken Charity's phone from her last night. I *knew* she was keeping something from me and Sandy. And this proves it. I–I think she knows where our daughter is hiding."

So did he. Not that Charity was hiding, but he was almost certain he knew where to find her. Although how she got there was a mystery. Surely she couldn't have driven that far? Maybe she caught a plane, but could she do that with Baxter? Probably. He was small enough still to travel as a carry-on.

Brody reached for the new journal once more and opened to the first page. He had to be sure. Hope surged as he scanned the words again.

Aunt Faith always knows how to make me feel better…

He was positive he was right.

"I–I think I know where Charity is, or where she's headed. Although if she's been gone for as long as you suspect, she could've arrived a few hours ago." If that was the case, why hadn't his sister called him?

It was a long shot, but the only one they had. If he was wrong… He didn't even want to think about being wrong. He couldn't wrap his mind around going down to the police station to report their daughter missing, and somehow dealing with the aftermath of what that would entail.

Brody placed the book on the bed then stretched out his leg and shoved his hand in his pants pocket to retrieve his phone. He dialed Faith's number.

He was about to hang up when she answered.

"Brody... I was just about to contact you." His sister sounded annoyed.

He put the phone on speaker so that Madison could also hear. His throat swelled with emotion, making it difficult for him to speak. Swallowing hard, he managed to stutter, "I–is she t–there? With you?"

Please God, let her be there.

CHAPTER EIGHTEEN

MADISON'S HEAD spun at the thought. Could Charity really be all the way in Colorado?

Faith's voice booming over the speaker quickly drew her back to the present. "You two have a *lot* of explaining to do."

In all the years that Madison had been married to Brody, she'd never heard his sister so angry. In fact, she'd never heard Faith angry, period. Not even when she had thought her husband was cheating on her.

"Faith, is Charity with you?" Madison reiterated Brody's question. But just because it seemed as if Faith knew something was up, it didn't mean that their daughter was there with her in Loveland.

"Yes. Charity is here with us. What on earth is going on?" Faith's tone was demanding and unsympathetic toward Brody and Madison. "Imagine my surprise when, just as I'm about to serve dinner, I see a yellow Volkswagen pull up in my driveway and my favorite niece—my *only* niece—climb out of the small car. Your child was on the road for ten hours, and you didn't even know she was missing? How could you be so clueless?"

In their defense, how could they have known? Still, if she had only driven home earlier that morning to check on Charity, she might've been able to stop her foolhardy quest. She couldn't believe that her daughter had driven across Kansas to the next state. Nearly six hundred miles.

Madison opened her mouth to speak then shut it. She had no words of explanation. Finally she asked, "H–how is she? I–is she okay?"

"What do you think?" Faith shot back. "She's exhausted from the journey, as is her puppy, and her heart is broken."

Of course, Baxter was with her. At least she hadn't been alone in the car. But the pup aside, hadn't Charity always said she'd never be alone because God was always with her?

Thank You for keeping my child safe.

"You should be ashamed of yourselves. And Brody… What in the world is wrong with you? How can you give up on your marriage over something as trivial as your wife's talent?"

Exactly! How could he? And not only had he given up on her, but his actions had caused their daughter to run away. Now that she knew their daughter was safe, the more she thought about the things Brody had done, the more her anger simmered.

Faith huffed. "You should be proud of Madison and want the world to see what she's capable of. Instead, it seems you're quite happy to hide her talents under the bushel called Peterson Galleries…choosing whom *you* wish to see her work." She was on a roll telling them off, especially Brody. There seemed there'd be no stopping her.

Brody's face contorted, and he shot back, "Because *he* did, and look where it got him!"

"He? You're talking in riddles, Brody. Who did what?" Faith seemed as confused by Brody's statement as Madison.

His face crumpled, and he yanked the elastic from his hair. He raked his fingers through the shoulder-length brown strands then inhaled deeply, his cheeks expanding like a blowfish as he exhaled the breath. "I–it's time you all learned the ugly t–truth."

Feeling sick to her stomach, Madison brushed a palm across his cheek, unable to shake the sense that the next words about to come out of Brody's mouth would change their lives forever.

And she had no idea whether it would be a change for the better, or for the worse.

Turning his head to face her, Madison's eyes searched his, her heart pounding from anger, fear, confusion. "What truth, Brody?"

At the same time, Faith asked the same question.

Brody leaned his head back to look at the ceiling as he wiped his hands over his face. He lowered his head to stare at the phone trembling in his hand. "D–dad. He did everything to encourage my mother's artistic talent, but it backfired on him, and he was left with a broken heart and a tiny babe to raise. Alone."

On the other side of the line, Faith choked. "Whoa… Back up a bit. What do you mean *your* mother? Our mom didn't have a creative bone in her body. She was the mathematician…always said I got my analytical brain from her. Besides, she *was* there for you, Brody. Wasn't she?"

What if their mother hadn't been? Brody was almost three years older than Faith. Who knew what happened in their parents' marriage during those first few years? Question was—how did Brody know? He couldn't possibly remember things he'd experienced when he was that young.

Brody rubbed his jaw with his free hand, exhaling yet another weighted sigh. "W–we don't have the same biological mother, Faith."

What?

"Dad was married before? You have a different mother?" Disbelief thickened Faith's words.

"To his shame, they never married, Dad always said. Even

though he'd desperately wanted to. That's why it was so much easier for my mom to walk out the door and leave—pursue her career, never look back."

Like pieces of a jigsaw puzzle fitting together, the picture became clearer, and Madison started to understand her husband's fears. This must have been so hard for him to speak about.

Her earlier anger began to ebb away, compassion taking its place.

If only she had known.

"I'm so sorry, Faith," Brody sobbed, wiping his eyes. "I never wanted you to know that we were only half-brother and sister. I–I thought you would love me less…maybe not love me at all."

"No! We are, and always will be, brother and sister. Nothing can change that, Brody. Nothing can diminish the love I have for you as my older brother."

Bless Faith's heart. She always knew the right thing to say.

Oh the turmoil Brody must've felt growing up, knowing he wasn't fully one of them. No wonder he had issues.

Madison's eyes teared up again at her husband's suffering. Just how long had he kept this secret? At least eight years, for sure—since before his parents' deaths. Maybe longer. Perhaps Brody's father had told him on his deathbed.

"D–do you know anything about her?" Faith asked. "If you're up to talking about it, that is. I'd really like to know, and I'm sure Madison would too, so that we can understand your pain."

Brody nodded to the screen, even though this wasn't a video call. "S–she was an aspiring artist—and yes, I take after her. There came a day, not that long into their relationship, when she got her big break. According to Dad, she said it was something she couldn't pursue with a six-month-old on the hip, one she had—" His voice broke and he hung his head. His loose hair swayed as he shook his head from side to side. Swallowing hard, he sucked in a breath. "…never bonded with anyway, who was merely a hindrance to her ability to create. So she walked out on Dad and me, and never looked back. Dad moved from Kansas to Colorado a year later where he met your…*our* mother. They soon married."

"Oh, Brody. I'm so sorry. I never knew." Faith sounded so contrite, and Madison was sure that had his sister known all of this when she'd answered his call, she would never have come down on Brody so harshly. "H–how long have you known? How did you find out?"

"I stumbled across my birth certificate when I was ten," Brody said, speaking a little easier now. Would confiding in them set him free from this lifetime of pain? "I couldn't understand why some other woman's name was on the document, so I confronted Mom and Dad later that night after dinner, when you and Tyler were in bed. Dad didn't tell me the whole ugly truth right away, but as I probed for answers over the years, he offered more and more details about my mother leaving me…leaving him. It was as painful for him to revisit that time in his life as it was for me to hear the truth.

"I–I've suffered with abandonment issues since I was a young boy. M–maybe that is why I am the way I am today—always trying to control, to keep people close to me, fearful of losing them…" His gaze sought Madison's, pleading with her to understand as he whispered, "I–I'm so sorry for all I've put you through. Please, forgive me."

Tears trailed down Madison's cheeks as she nodded. Her going to New York and taking Charity with her must've seemed like the biggest betrayal for Brody. No wonder he'd reacted the way he had. It was starting to make sense now.

Faith's soft voice soothed. "You need help to overcome those feelings of rejection, Brody. For yourself, but mostly to save your crumbling marriage. And the first place you need to start is in your relationship with God."

She took a deep breath. "I know that I told you the other day I wouldn't preach to you, but I'm sorry, I need to make an exception because what I'm about to say, needs to be said. So please, grant me the soapbox just this once."

Brody's Adam's apple bobbed up and down as he swallowed. "Go on."

Faith didn't hesitate. "Would it help you to know that Jesus, the Son of God, felt abandoned too?"

Brody's brows arched upward. "He did?"

"Yes. On the cross when He was crucified for our sins, He cried out to His Father, 'My God, my God, why have You forsaken me?'"

Faith's words penetrated deep into Madison's soul. And by the look on Brody's face, his too.

"And then He cried out again," Faith continued. "Likely the same anguished question, before He blew out His final breath. Jesus died feeling forsaken by the most important person in His life—His Father. He knows how you're feeling, Brody. But He conquered death. He conquered sin. And He conquered that abandonment, *your* abandonment, on the cross. He has said that He will *never* leave us, *never* forsake us."

Madison cracked a smile. That was Charity's favorite verse.

"Brody…Madison… For too long you've been painting your own pictures of what your life should be like. Why don't you put your palettes down and let the Master artist finish the canvas of your life? Allow Him to create the masterpiece you both never could."

"I–I'd like that." Brody glanced at Madison.

She nodded. "So would I."

With a smile that spoke of a weight lifting from Brody, he said, "Faith, would you help Madison and me to pray…" He turned to

Madison. "What did Charity's pastor call it?"

"The sinner's prayer." Madison remembered Pastor Andy praying that prayer at the end of every service, inviting anyone in the congregation to say the words after him.

The strangest feeling of excitement welled up in Madison's chest. She clasped Brody's hand tightly and leaned on his shoulder. Their lives *were* about to change, but there was no doubt in her mind that it would be for the better.

Far, far better.

Before Madison and Brody bade farewell to a traumatic day, they knelt beside their bed and prayed together for the very first time, thanking God for their daughter's safety, and for His relentless love in pursuing them and bringing them salvation. They had spent the evening confessing the things they'd done to each other, asking each other for forgiveness, making things right. Madison had never felt as close to her husband. And more importantly, to God. She loved it and wanted to savor this feeling every day of her life.

As they slid between the sheets, Brody reached out to retrieve the Bible they'd borrowed from the collection Charity had in her room. Tomorrow, they would go out and buy their own so that they could write in them and make bright-colored highlights—just as Charity was fond of doing. After all, they were artists and they loved painting their world with color.

Brody kissed her head and opened the Bible to the middle. "Where should we start?"

Madison turned to him and smiled. She loved this man so much. "Usually I'd say at the beginning, but Faith suggested we start at the book of John in the New Testament…not first John, remember."

Brody chuckled. "I remember."

He flipped back to the index in the front then trailed a finger down the New Testament books until he found John. He turned to the page indicated and began reading aloud. "In the beginning was the Word, and the Word was with God, and the Word was God. He was with God in the beginning. Through him all things were made; without him nothing was made that has been made. In him was life, and that life was the light of all mankind. The light shines in the darkness, and the darkness has not overcome it."

They took turns reading one chapter each, until it was Madison's turn to read chapter six. Jesus feeds the five thousand. Madison looked forward to that one, but she was also tired. It had been a draining day.

A yawn slipped from her mouth, and she covered her mouth to hide it.

"You're tired. We should get some sleep." Brody closed the Bible. He set it down on the nightstand then turned out the light. Moonlight filtered in through the windows, the curtains not drawn. "We can read more tomorrow, all right?"

Madison nodded and snuggled into his arms, once again feeling the need to set things right. She was certain with time they'd both learn to fully forgive each other, and themselves. "Brody, again, I'm so sorry for all I've done to increase your anxieties."

"My love, you never knew. And I should have told you all a long, long time ago. I should have told everyone. I feel so free since I exposed the secret I've lived with for thirty-four long years, like this gigantic burden has rolled away. Please forgive me for not trusting you with that part of me."

Reaching up, she planted a soft kiss on his lips. "I forgive you."

Brody tightened his embrace and rested his head on Madison's.

One thing still weighed on her mind. Brody hadn't said if he knew who his mother was, or if he'd ever met her. In the light of their newfound transparency, she would ask rather than live with uncertainty and secrets again.

"Brody," she whispered. "Do you know who your mother is? Did you ever get to meet her?"

He sucked in a deep breath, his chest rising as he filled his lungs. "My whole life I've worked and strived to be worthy of my mother's love, thinking that perhaps she would notice and reach out to me. She never did."

So he did know who she was.

"According to my birth certificate, my mother's name was Eleanor Sanderson. But the world, especially the art world, knows her as Ellie Sanders."

Madison shot upright and stared at her husband. She couldn't have been more shocked if Brody had dumped a bucket of cold water over her head. No wonder he was so adamant she didn't go. How much deeper he must've felt betrayed than she'd first thought.

That's why Ellie Sanders had looked so familiar to her when they first met in person. How had she not seen the resemblance between her and Brody? And as for Ellie's comment about Charity's eyes being like her father's… Without a doubt, the woman knew that Brody was her son. But Madison couldn't tell her husband that. Not now. One day, though, when the time was right, she would.

"I…"

"It's all right," he soothed. "How could you have known?"

This shone an entirely different light on everything.

She laced her fingers in his. "I won't take part in the exhibition, Brody. I'll withdraw. Give the money back. Let them give the first place to Georgia Bell. She's a worthy winner."

Brody reached out and tucked her hair behind her ear, his touch gentle, his expression overflowing with compassion—not the my-way-or-the-highway looks she had grown so accustomed to over the years.

"No, babe. You deserve to be there. I want you to go. As you said, it's an incredible opportunity—I can't deny that. You and Charity must go, and I will be right there beside you to support you this time." He huffed a laugh. "Seeing as I'm facing my demons, I guess it's time I faced my biological mother too."

Madison squeezed his hand to reassure him. "I want you to be reassured of one thing, Brody—I am not your mother. I'm not going anywhere after this exhibition. My life is here in this sleepy hollow with you and Charity. If more people want my work, let them come to Peterson Galleries."

Dear Jesus

What a faithful God You are. My heart has gone from broken to overflowing with gratitude in the space of a day.

Thank You for bringing me to Aunt Faith's house safely. I admit, it was daunting to drive so far and took so much longer than usual because of all the pit stops I had to make for Baxter. And, of course, I don't drive nearly as fast as all the other cars. But I got here in one piece, and I'm so thankful. You were with me all the way.

Thank You for the spare prayer journal Aunt Faith gave me— my other one only has six entries, but I'll add all that I pen during my time in Colorado to that journal once I'm home. Thank You that You work everything for good. If mine hadn't slid unnoticed from my bag back home, Mom and Dad might not have come to know You. And oh, what a party there must be in heaven tonight because they have been hard nuts to crack. But You, Lord...You make everything beautiful in its time. And You have done just that for my Mom and Dad. Now that they have You in their lives, I know they're gonna make it. Dad even said how sorry he was for asking Mom to leave the house, and for the way he'd treated both her and me when we were in New York, and asked me to please forgive him for being such a jerk so many times. So even though they have a lot to work through, I know they're going to do so by looking to You for guidance—I could just hear in in their voices when I spoke to them earlier.

Thank You that Mom and Dad have allowed me to stay on for a short while with Aunt Faith before they fly over next weekend to fetch me. It's good, because I think they need the time alone to get closer to each other again, and to get close to You. There is much they want to tell me, but they want to do so face-to-face. So I'll wait patiently until I see them.

Jesus, You have been my strength through this ordeal. So have Aunt Faith and Aunt Hope. Those incredible women have both been through so much, but because of You, they've survived.

Ha, when I told Aunt Faith that, she smiled and said, "Survivors, yes, that's what we are. And so will you be. You know the Bible says that when all is said and done, that there are three things that remain: Faith, Hope, and Charity."

I reminded her that the greatest of those was Charity.

I know You know all of this, but I'm writing it down so that I don't forget...

All my love
Your forever grateful favorite
Charity

P.S. And thank You for giving me such a good friend in Melinda. I can't believe she was willing to sit at my house all day to cover for me. I am sorry I had to deceive everyone.

CHAPTER NINETEEN

Three weeks later…

BRODY TUGGED at the neck of his collar, trying to give himself room to breathe. He inhaled a lungful of air as the chauffeur pulled the white stretch limousine to a stop outside the Ellie Sanders Gallery in the center of Manhattan.

The chauffeur climbed out of the vehicle and opened the back door. Brody eased out first then helped Madison and Charity. Stepping aside, he allowed the chauffeur to assist his mother and father-in-law.

Madison straightened his bow tie then brushed the shoulders of his tux. "You okay?"

He nodded. "I'll be fine."

Would he? His heart whacked against his chest with every beat. Even though Pastor Andy's counseling had helped Brody immensely, to the point that he felt he could cope with this day, it was still difficult to control the palpitations. Forgiving your mother for a lifetime of rejection wasn't easy. But with God's help, it *was* possible.

Every time he allowed the Lord to wash away a little more of the hurt, God painted another corner of His masterpiece titled *Brody Peterson*.

The gallery was magnificent inside. Double volume with bright spotlights that shone down from an industrial-style roof. On the sides, high white walls stretched from the floor to the roof, and inside the gallery, panels of the same height—some four foot wide, others longer—staggered their way through the room, far enough apart from each other so that the patrons could see several artworks at once. Twenty-five of Madison's pieces were displayed on those walls tonight—*Girl in a Field* in the prime spot and the very first canvas to be seen.

Around the beechwood floor with its soft reddish grain, art enthusiasts rubbed shoulders. The party was already buzzing. All it lacked was its guest of honor.

An elegant woman in her sixties—wearing a long, figure-hugging black dress—sashayed toward them, her platinum blond hair swept back in a coiffured style.

Brody recognized her instantly.

Ellie Sanders.

His biological mother.

The moment surreal, he had to remind himself to breathe. How often he had dreamed of meeting her one day and of being able to boast of his own achievements. Now none of that mattered anymore. He wished but one thing—to hear from her if it had been worth it, whether she lived with any regrets over her decision?

"Madison, my dear." Ellie leaned forward and kissed Madison on one cheek, then the other. She turned and brushed a hand over Charity's head, stroking her palm down her granddaughter's hair. Did she know? "And sweet Charity. How are those beautiful wheat fields looking over in Kansas?"

Looking more woman than teen in the new white gown that she had chosen with Madison for this auspicious occasion, Charity grinned. "As the Bible says, Ms. Sanders, the wheat is ripe for harvest. And soon, the sunflower fields will be ready too."

"Oh… You're religious. How quaint." Ellie turned her attention from Charity to Brody. He was certain that if she hadn't, Charity would've politely told her that she wasn't religious, she was a follower of Jesus.

Ellie held out her hand examining—no, more like scrutinizing—him from top to toe. "And you must be Madison's charming husband. I do love your man ponytail. It's so artsy."

Brody laughed. "My wife thinks so too." He took Ellie's hand and kissed the top of it. "I'm Brody." His gaze locked with his mothers' for longer than what was normal.

It was uncanny to see her up close, the resemblance between them unmistakable. He had her same icy-blue eyes, her V-shaped nose, and her thin, straight lips. He was his mother's son all right.

Except, he wasn't.

Did she know who he was?

How could she not? His name, surname, career… His looks so like hers. But if she did, she wasn't letting on.

A wide smile brightened Ellie's face, accentuating the tiny wrinkles around her eyes. "Brody Peterson… Well, it certainly is a pleasure to meet you."

He would've liked to say the pleasure was his too, but Brody wasn't so sure this was pleasurable. Instead he kept his composure and nonchalantly responded, "You have a magnificent gallery, Ms. Sanders. Peterson Galleries pales in comparison." Unpleasant or not, Brody was determined to engage her in conversation to find a chance to ask the one question burning on his lips.

"It's taken many years of hard work and sacrifice. You're still young, Brody—you'll get there. And, of course, my endorsement of your wife's work won't hurt either." She paused then touched his arm. "You don't mind if I call you that, do you? Or would you prefer the formalities of Mr. Peterson."

He couldn't help smiling at that. His own mother calling him by something other than his first name. "Brody is fine."

"Then I insist you call me Ellie. None of this Ms. Sanders stuff."

A waitress dressed in black strolled past bearing a tray of tall flutes bubbling with champagne. Ellie stopped her and took two glasses. She handed one to Madison and the other to Brody before snagging one for herself. She glanced at Charity. "As for you, young lady... We'll need to find you a fruit juice." She looked at the waitress, one eyebrow raised. Immediately, the young woman scurried off to do Ellie's bidding without her even saying a word. This woman who bore him was certainly a formidable force.

"I suppose you must have made many sacrifices along the way. A husband...family...?" Brody stared at her, challenging her for an honest answer.

"I have." She sighed. "But, I made my choices a long time ago. Whether right or wrong, I've learned to live with them."

She took a sip of champagne. "I should mingle with the other guests. And so should you." She turned to go.

Brody reached out and grasped her by the arm.

She paused, twisting to look back at him.

"O—one more question before you disappear into the crowd." Brody's voice trembled and his eyes burned. "W—was it worth it?"

Ellie looked around the gallery that oozed wealth, then back at Brody. Her mouth turned in a wistful smile. "You tell me, Brody."

Although Ellie Sanders had given no indication during that brief interlude that she knew who he was, somehow Brody suspected that she did. Perhaps it was her social standing in the art world that had prevented her all these years from publically acknowledging him. Maybe now that she had met her son, she would throw caution to the wind and want to get to know him.

Strangely, he hoped that one day she would.

But Brody refused to lose any sleep if she didn't. With or without a mother, his life was complete because he knew beyond a shadow of a doubt, that he was loved and accepted by his wife, his child, and his siblings. Most of all, he was loved and accepted by Almighty God. And *that* was all that mattered.

Setting the empty champagne glass down on a passing tray, he linked one arm in Charity's, the other in Madison's and flashed them each a wide grin. "Come, my fair ladies. This is *your* night. Your fans await."

"Oh, before we go, Dad, can I make a request?" Charity flashed Brody a grin.

"Of course," both Brody and Madison said.

"Is it too early to tell you what I'd like for Christmas?"

Brody gazed down at his beautiful daughter, so grateful for her enduring faith and prayers that had brought them through the valley and onto the highest mountaintop. "It's never too early to make a Christmas list, Charity honey. So what is it that you'd like? Because you know your mother's career is about to skyrocket."

Charity laughed softly. "All I want is my own French easel, palette, some brushes, paint, and canvases. I'd like to try my hand at oil painting, I think."

"In that case, Christmas can come early this year." Brody smiled and walked his two special ladies into the room with confidence, thankful for the knowledge that with God and them at his side, he could face anything the world threw at him.

Even a mother who may, or may not, ever love him.

You, O Lord, have turned my mourning into dancing.

THE END

GLOSSARY

Barrel roof : A roof or ceiling having a semi-cylindrical form

Cheval mirror : A full-length mirror in a frame in which it may be tilted

Compass rose : [Navigation] A circle divided into 32 points or 360° numbered clockwise from true or magnetic north, printed on a chart or the like as a means of determining the course of a vessel or aircraft; a similar design, often ornamented, used on maps to indicate the points of the compass

F0 : Gale tornado, wind speed 40-72 mph

French easel : French easels are for the traveling artist. They contain a sketchbox, an easel, and a canvas carrier in a smaller package. The sketchbox holds paint supplies and a palette. The legs and canvas arm on a French easel collapse for ease of travel. French easels are excellent for painting outdoors.

GDL : Graduated Driver's License

Glamping : The activity of camping with some of the comforts and luxuries of home

Impasto : The laying on of paint thickly, painting technique [Italian]

Madder : Any plant of the genus Rubia, especially the climbing

R. tinctorum, of Europe, having open clusters of small, yellowish flowers; the root of this plant, formerly used in dyeing; the dye or coloring matter itself; a color produced by such a dye

Mammatus : Meaning "mammary cloud", is a cellular pattern of pouches hanging underneath the base of a cloud, typically cumulonimbus rainclouds, although they may be attached to other classes of parent clouds. Name derived from the Latin *mamma* (meaning "udder" or "breast").
[Wikipedia – https://creativecommons.org/licenses/by-sa/3.0/]

MCI : IATA code for Kansas City International Airport (originally Mid-Continent International Airport) is a public airport 15 miles northwest of downtown Kansas City in Platte County, Missouri

Nascar : The National Association for Stock Car Auto Racing (NASCAR) is an American auto racing sanctioning and operating company that is best known for stock-car racing

Prestissimo : In as fast a tempo as possible (Music)

TLC : Tender loving care

Scripture References

Chapter 3:

Therefore, in order to keep me from becoming conceited, I was given a thorn in my flesh, a messenger of Satan, to torment me. Three times I pleaded with the Lord to take it away from me. But he said to me, "My grace is sufficient for you, for my power is made perfect in weakness." Therefore I will boast all the more gladly about my weaknesses, so that Christ's power may rest on me. That is why, for Christ's sake, I delight in weaknesses, in insults, in hardships, in persecutions, in difficulties. For when I am weak, then I am strong
~ 2 Corinthians 12 v 7-10 (NIV)

Chapter 5:

Be angry and do not sin; do not let the sun go down on your anger.
~ Ephesians 4 v 26 (NIV)

Chapter 14 & 15:

"Therefore I tell you, do not worry about your life, what you will eat or drink; or about your body, what you will wear. Is not life more than food, and the body more than clothes? Look at the birds of the air; they do not sow or reap or store away in barns, and yet your heavenly Father feeds them. Are you not much more valuable than they? Can any one of you by worrying add a single hour to your life?

"And why do you worry about clothes? See how the flowers of the field grow. They do not labor or spin. Yet I tell you that not even Solomon in all his splendor was dressed like one of these. If that is how God clothes the grass of the field, which is here today and tomorrow is thrown into the fire, will he not much more clothe you—you of little faith? So do not worry, saying, 'What shall we eat?' or 'What shall we drink?' or 'What shall we wear?' For the pagans run after all these things, and your heavenly Father knows that you need them. But seek first his kingdom and his righteousness, and all these things will be given to you as well.

Therefore do not worry about tomorrow, for tomorrow will worry about itself. Each day has enough trouble of its own."
~ Matthew 6 v 25-34 (NIV)

And we know that all things work together for good to them that love God, to them who are the called according to his purpose.
~ Romans 8 v 28 (NIV)

Chapter 15:

You keep track of all my sorrows. You have collected all my tears in your bottle. You have recorded each one in your book.
~ Psalm 56 v 8 (NLT)

Children, obey your parents in the Lord, for this is right.
~ Ephesians 6 v 1 (NIV)

Chapter 18:

"Never will I leave you; never will I forsake you."
~ Hebrews 13 v 5 (NIV)

About three in the afternoon Jesus cried out in a loud voice, "Eli, Eli, lema sabachthani?" (which means "My God, my God, why have you forsaken me?").

And when Jesus had cried out again in a loud voice, he gave up his spirit.
~ Matthew 27 v 46 & 50 (NIV)

In the beginning was the Word, and the Word was with God, and the Word was God. He was with God in the beginning. Through him all things were made; without him nothing was made that has been made. In him was life, and that life was the light of all mankind. The light shines in the darkness, and the darkness has not overcome it.
~ John 1 v 1-5 (NIV)

He has made everything beautiful in its time. He has also set eternity in the human heart; yet no one can fathom what God has done from beginning to end.
~ Ecclesiastes 3 v 11 (NIV)

And now there remain faith, hope, and charity, these three: but the greatest of these is charity.
~ 1 Corinthians 13 v 13 (DRA)

Chapter 19:

Don't you have a saying, 'It's still four months until harvest'? I tell you, open your eyes and look at the fields! They are ripe for harvest.
~ John 4 v 35 (NIV)

You have turned my mourning into joyful dancing. You have taken away my clothes of mourning and clothed me with joy.
~ Psalm 30 v 11

I hope you enjoyed reading *Reclaiming Charity*. If you did, please consider leaving a short review on Amazon, Goodreads, or Bookbub. Positive reviews and word-of-mouth recommendations count as they honor an author and help other readers to find quality Christian fiction to read.

Thank you so much!

If you enjoyed this book, you might like to read the other two books in this series, *Restoring Faith* (Shaped by Love - Book 1) and *Recovering Hope* (Shaped by Love - Book 2).

See The Potter's House Books for more details, http://pottershousebooks.com/

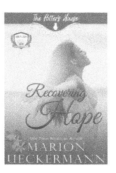

If you'd like to receive information on new releases, cover reveals, and writing news, please sign up for my newsletter.

http://www.marionueckermann.net/subscribe/

ABOUT MARION UECKERMANN

A Novel place to Fall in love

USA Today bestselling author MARION UECKERMANN's passion for writing was sparked when she moved to Ireland with her family. Her love of travel has influenced her contemporary inspirational romances set in novel places. Marion and her husband again live in South Africa and are setting their sights on retirement when they can join their family in the beautiful Cape.

Please visit Marion's website for more of her books:
www.marionueckermann.net

You can also find Marion on social media:
Facebook : Marion.C.Ueckermann
Twitter : ueckie
Goodreads : 5342167.Marion_Ueckermann
Pinterest : ueckie
Bookbub : authors/marion-ueckermann
Amazon : Marion-Ueckermann/e/B00KBYLU7C

TITLES BY MARION UECKERMANN

CONTEMPORARY CHRISTIAN ROMANCE

CHAPEL COVE ROMANCES
Remember Me *(Book 1)*
Choose Me *(Book 4)*
Accept Me *(Book 8)*
Trust Me *(Book 10)*
Releasing 2020
Other books in this tri-author series are by
Alexa Verde and Autumn Macarthur

THE POTTER'S HOUSE
Restoring Faith *(Shaped by Love - Book 1)*
Recovering Hope *(Shaped by Love - Book 2)*
Reclaiming Charity *(Shaped by Love - Book 3)*

A TUSCAN LEGACY
That's Amore *(Book 1)*
Ti Amo *(Book 4)*
Other books in this multi-author series are by: Elizabeth Maddrey, Alexa Verde, Clare
Revell, Heather Gray, Narelle Atkins, and Autumn Macarthur

UNDER THE SUN
SEASONS OF CHANGE
A Time to Laugh *(Book 1)*
A Time to Love *(Book 2)*
A Time to Push Daisies *(Book 3)*

HEART OF ENGLAND
SEVEN SUITORS FOR SEVEN SISTERS
A Match for Magnolia *(Book 1)*
A Romance for Rose *(Book 2)*
A Hero for Heather *(Book 3)*
A Husband for Holly *(Book 4)*
A Courtship for Clover *(Book 5)*
A Proposal for Poppy *(Book 6 - Releasing 2020)*
A Love for Lily *(Book 7 - Releasing 2021)*

HEART OF AFRICA
Orphaned Hearts
The Other You

HEART OF IRELAND
Spring's Promise

HEART OF AUSTRALIA
Melbourne Memories

HEART OF CHRISTMAS
Poles Apart
Ginger & Brad's House

PASSPORT TO ROMANCE
Helsinki Sunrise
Soloppgang i Helsinki
(Norwegian translation of Helsinki Sunrise)
Oslo Overtures
Glasgow Grace

ACFW WRITERS ON THE STORM
SHORT STORY CONTEST WINNERS ANTHOLOGY
Dancing Up A Storm ~ *Dancing In The Rain*

NON-FICTION
Bush Tails
(Humorous & True Short Story Trophies of my Bushveld Escapades
as told by Percival Robert Morrison)

POETRY

Glimpses Through Poetry
[Bumper paperback of the four e-book poetry collections below]

GLIMPSES THROUGH POETRY
My Father's Hand
My Savior's Touch
My Colorful Life

WORDS RIPE FOR THE PICKING
Fruit of the Rhyme

When love grows cold and vows forgotten, can faith be restored?

Charles and Faith Young are numbers people. While Charles spends his days in a fancy Fort Collins office number crunching, Faith teaches math to the students of Colorado High. Married for sixteen years, Charles and Faith both know unequivocally that one plus one should never equal three.

When blame becomes the order of the day in the Young household for their failing marriage—blaming each other, blaming themselves—Charles and Faith each search for answers why the flame of love no longer burns brightly. In their efforts, one takes comfort from another a step too far. One chooses not to get mad, but to get even.

Dying love is a slow burn. Is it too late for Charles and Faith to fan the embers and make love rise once again from the ashes of their broken marriage? Can they find their first love again—for each other, and for God?

In a single moment, a dream dies, and hope is lost.

Lovers of the ocean, Hope and Tyler Peterson long for the day they can dip their little one's feet into its clear blue waters and pass on their passion for the sea.

Despite dedicating her life to the rescue and rehabilitation of God's sea creatures, when their dream dies, Hope can't muster the strength to do the same for herself. Give her a dark hole to hide away from the world and she'd be happy…if happiness were ever again within her reach.

While Tyler is able to design technology that probes the mysteries of the deep, he's at a loss to find a way to help Hope surface from the darkness that has dragged her into its abyss. He struggles to plan for their future when his wife can barely cope with the here and now.

If they can't recover hope, their marriage won't survive.

What she most needed was right there in front of her all along.

At the age of thirteen, Clarise Aylward and her two best friends each pen a wish list of things they want to achieve. Deciding to bury a tin containing their life goals, the friends vow to unearth the metal box once they've all turned forty. But as the decades pass and each girl chases her dreams, the lists are forgotten.

Heath Brock has been in love with Clarise for over twenty-seven years and counting. As a young man, he'd plucked up the courage to ask her out on a Valentine's date, but the couple succumbed to pent-up passions, sending Clarise dashing for the other side of the country.

Years after Clarise's sudden departure, Heath serves as youth pastor. He'd held out hope of Clarise's return, but buries his feelings for his childhood sweetheart when he learns she's married.

Almost penniless, divorced, and with nowhere to go, Clarise returns home to Chapel Cove, her future uncertain. She's approaching forty with her dreams in tatters. When old feelings resurface, Clarise wonders whether she's ever really fallen out of love with Heath.

What's the man of God to do when his old flame returns, seemingly to stay?

With Clarise back in town, Heath is determined not to repeat past mistakes, but if he has anything to say about it, never again will he lose the only woman he's ever loved.

The one thing he wants most in the world, she can't give him.

Her heart broken at the altar, real estate agent Julia Delpont moves south to Chapel Cove, away from the humiliation, the gossip, the stares. At least in this small town, nobody knew her story. And she had every intention of keeping it that way. No man would ever break her heart again.

After three years as an army surgeon in war-torn Afghanistan, Dr. Hudson Brock avoids the ER, choosing instead to perform scheduled surgeries at a top Dallas hospital. But neither extreme in his career has offered Hudson what he really wants—a wife and family to come home to at night. Maybe in the sleepy hollow town he'd grown up in he would find what he was looking for.

Once back in Chapel Cove, Hudson tries to find the perfect house. He suspects that finding the perfect woman will take far longer.

When Julia Delpont literally stumbles into Hudson's life, he knows he's the one who has fallen harder. But Julia is afraid to open her heart again. Especially to the handsome doctor whose deepest desires she cannot fill.

She came seeking her mother. She found so much more.

On her deathbed, Haddie Hayes's mother whispers a secret into Haddie's ear—one that she and Haddie's father had kept for twenty-eight years. The truth that Haddie wasn't born a Hayes sends this shy Kentucky girl far from the bluegrass of home to a small coastal town in Oregon in search of her birth mother. Hopefully in Chapel Cove she'll find the answers to all her questions.

EMT Riley Jordan can't help himself—he's a fixer, a helper, sometimes to his own detriment. A 911 call to Ivy's on Spruce has Riley attending to Haddie Hayes, the new girl in town. After Riley learns of Haddie's quest, he promises to help her find her birth family.

When Haddie makes the wrong assumptions, she vows to give up on her foolish crusade and go back to the only place she called home, a place she'd always felt safe and loved. But a freak accident hinders her plans of bolting from Chapel Cove.

And running from Riley…who has a secret of his own.

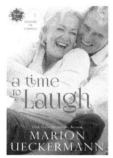

For thirty years, Brian and Elizabeth Dunham have served on the mission field. Unable to have children of their own, they've been a father and mother to countless orphans in six African countries. When an unexpected beach-house inheritance and a lung disease diagnosis coincide, they realize that perhaps God is telling them it's time to retire.

At sixty, Elizabeth is past child-bearing age. She'd long ago given up wondering whether this would be the month she would conceive. But when her best friend and neighbor jokes that Elizabeth's sudden fatigue and nausea are symptoms of pregnancy, Elizabeth finds herself walking that familiar and unwanted road again, wondering if God is pulling an Abraham and Sarah on her and Brian.

The mere notion has questions flooding Elizabeth's mind. If she were miraculously pregnant, would they have the stamina to raise a child in their golden years? Especially with Brian's health issues. And the child? Would it be healthy, or would it go through life struggling with some kind of disability? What of her own health? Could she survive giving birth?

Will what Brian and Elizabeth have dreamed of their entire married life be an old-age blessing or a curse?

Everyday life for Dr. Melanie Kerr had consisted of happy deliveries and bundles of joy…until her worst nightmare became reality. The first deaths in her OR during an emergency C-section. Both mother and child, one month before Christmas. About to perform her first Caesarean since the tragedy, Melanie loses her nerve and flees the OR. She packs her bags and catches a flight to Budapest. Perhaps time spent in the city her lost patient hailed from, can help her find the healing and peace she desperately needs to be a good doctor again.

Since the filming of Jordan's Journeys' hit TV serial "Life Begins at Sixty" ended earlier in the year, journalist and TV host Jordan Stanson has gone from one assignment to the next. But before he can take a break, he has a final episode to film—"Zac's First Christmas". Not only is he looking forward to relaxing at his parents' seaside home, he can't wait to see his godchild, Zac, the baby born to the aging Dunhams. His boss, however, has squeezed in another documentary for him to complete before Christmas—uncovering the tragedy surrounding the doctor the country came to love on his show, the beautiful Dr. Kerr.

In order to chronicle her journey through grief and failure, Jordan has no choice but to get close to this woman. Something he has both tried and failed at in the past. He hopes through this assignment, he'll be able to help her realize the tragedy wasn't her fault. But even in a city so far away from home, work once again becomes the major catalyst to hinder romance between Jordan and Melanie.

That, and a thing called honesty.

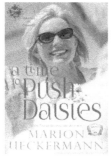

Not every woman is fortunate enough to find her soulmate. Fewer find him twice.

JoAnn Stanson has loved and lost. Widowed a mere eighteen months ago, JoAnn is less than thrilled when her son arranges a luxury cruise around the British Isles as an early birthday gift. She's not ready to move on and "meet new people".

Caleb Blume has faced death and won. Had it not been for an unexpected Christmas present, he would surely have been pushing up daisies. Not that the silver-haired landscape architect was averse to those little flowers—he just wasn't ready to become fertilizer himself.

To celebrate his sixty-fourth birthday and the nearing two-year anniversary since he'd cheated death, Caleb books a cruise and flies to London. He is instantly drawn in a way that's never happened before to a woman he sees boarding the ship. But this woman who steals Caleb's heart is far more guarded with her own. For JoAnn, so many little things about Caleb remind her of her late husband. It's like loving the same man twice. Yet different.

When Rafaele and Jayne meet again two years after dancing the night away together in Tuscany, is it a matter of fate or of faith?

After deciding to take a six-month sabbatical, Italian lawyer Rafaele Rossi moves from Florence back to Villa Rossi in the middle of Tuscany, resigned to managing the family farm for his aging nonna after his father's passing. Convinced a family get-together is what Nonna needs to lift her spirits, he plans an eightieth birthday party for her, making sure his siblings and cousins attend.

The Keswick jewelry store where Jayne Austin has worked for seven years closes its doors. Jayne takes her generous severance pay and heads off to Italy—Tuscany to be precise. Choosing to leave her fate in God's hands, she prays she'll miraculously bump into the handsome best man she'd danced the night away with at a friend's Tuscan wedding two years ago. She hasn't been able to forget those smoldering brown eyes and that rich Italian accent.

Jayne's prayers are answered swiftly and in the most unexpected way. Before she knows what's happening, she's a guest not only at Isabella Rossi's birthday party, but at Villa Rossi too.

When Rafaele receives what appears to be a valuable painting from an unknown benefactor, he's reminded that he doesn't want to lose Jayne again. After what he's done to drive her from the villa, though, what kind of a commitment will it take for her to stay?

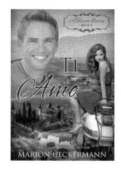

She never wants to get married. He does. To her.

The day Alessandra Rossi was born, her mammà died, and a loveless life with the father who blamed the newborn for her mother's death followed. With the help of her oldest brother, Rafaele, Alessa moved away from home the moment she finished school— just like her other siblings had. Now sporting a degree in architectural history and archaeology, Alessa loves her job as a tour guide in the city of Rome—a place where she never fails to draw the attention of men. Not that Alessa cares. Fearing that the man she weds would be anything like her recently deceased father has Alessa vowing to remain single.

American missionary Michael Young has moved to Rome on a two-year mission trip. His temporary future in the country doesn't stop him from spontaneously joining Alessa's tour after spotting her outside the Colosseum. *And* being bold enough to tell her afterward that one day she'd be his wife. God had told him. And he believed Him. But Alessa shows no sign of interest in Michael.

Can anything sway the beautiful and headstrong Italian to fall in love? Can anyone convince her to put her faith and hope in the Heavenly Father, despite being raised by an earthly one who never loved her? Will her sister's prompting, or a mysterious painting, or Michael himself change Alessa's mind? About love. And about God.

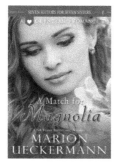

Womanizer. Adulterer. Divorced. That is Lord Davis Rathbone's history. His future? He vows to never marry or fall in love again—repeating his past mistakes, not worth the risk. Then he meets Magnolia Blume, and filling his days penning poetry no longer seems an alternative to channel his pent-up feelings. With God's help, surely he can keep this rare treasure and make it work this time?

Magnolia Blume's life is perfect, except for one thing—Davis Rathbone is everything she's not looking for in a man. He doesn't strike her as one prone to the sentiments of family, or religion, but her judgments could be premature.

Magnolia must look beyond the gossip, Davis's past, and their differences to find her perfect match, because, although flawed, Davis has one redeeming quality—he is a man after God's own heart.

Rose Blume has a secret, and she's kept it for six long years. It's the reason she's convinced herself she'll have to find her joy making wedding dresses, and not wearing one.

Fashion design icon Joseph Digiavoni crosses paths with Rose for the first time since their summer romance in Florence years before, and all the old feelings for her come rushing back. Not that they ever really left. He's lived with her image since she returned to England.

Joseph and Rose are plunged into working together on the wedding outfits for the upcoming Rathbone / Blume wedding. His top client is marrying Rose's sister. But will this task prove too difficult, especially when Joseph is anxious for Rose to admit why she broke up with him in Italy and what she'd done in the months that followed?

One person holds the key to happiness for them all, if only Rose and

Joseph trusted that the truth would set them free. When they finally do bare their secrets, who has the most to forgive?

Paxton Rathbone is desperate to make his way home. His inheritance long spent, he stows away on a fishing trawler bound from Norway to England only to be discovered, beaten and discarded at Scarborough's port. On home soil at last, all it would take is one phone call. But even if his mother and father are forgiving, he doubts his older brother will be.

Needing a respite from child welfare social work, Heather Blume is excited about a short-term opportunity to work at a busy North Yorkshire day center for the homeless. When one of the men she's been helping saves her from a vicious attack, she's so grateful she violates one of the most important rules in her profession—she takes him home to tend his wounds. But there's more to her actions than merely being the Good Samaritan. The man's upper-crust speech has Heather intrigued. She has no doubt he's a gentleman fallen far from grace and is determined to reunite the enigmatic young man with his family, if only he would open up about his life.

Paxton has grown too accustomed to the disdain of mankind, which perhaps is why Heather's kindness penetrates his reserves and gives him reason to hope. Reason to love? Perhaps reason to stay. But there's a fine line between love and gratitude, for both Paxton and Heather.

Holly Blume loves decorating people's homes, but that doesn't mean she's ready to play house.

Believing a house is not a home without a woman's touch, there's nothing more Reverend Christopher Stewart would like than to find a wife. What woman would consider him marriage material, though, with an aging widowed father to look after, especially one who suffers from Alzheimer's?

When Christopher arrives at his new parish, he discovers the church ladies have arranged a welcome surprise—an office makeover by congregant and interior designer Holly Blume. Impressed with Miss Blume's work, Christopher decides to contract the talented lady to turn the rectory into a home. When they begin to clash more than their taste in color, will the revamp come to the same abrupt end as his only romantic relationship?

Despite their differences, Holly resolves to finish the job of redesigning the Stewart home, while Christopher determines to re-form Holly's heart.

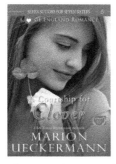

Top London chef Clover Blume has one chance to become better acquainted with Jonathan Spalding away from the mayhem of her busy restaurant where he frequently dines—usually with a gorgeous woman at his side. When the groomsman who is supposed to escort her at her sister's New Year's Eve wedding is delayed because of business, Clover begins to wonder whether she really wants to waste time with a player whose main focus in life is making money rather than keeping promises.

Jonathan lives the good life. There's one thing, however, the London Investment Banker's money hasn't managed to buy: a woman to love— one worthy of his mother's approval. Is it possible though, that the auburn-haired beauty who is to partner with him at his best friend's wedding—a wedding he stands to miss thanks to a glitch in a deal worth millions—is finding a way into his heart?

But what will it cost Jonathan to realize it profits him nothing to gain the world, yet lose his soul?

And the girl.

Who am I? The question has Taylor Cassidy journeying from one side of America to the other seeking an answer. Almost five years brings her no closer to the truth. Now an award-winning photojournalist for Wines & Vines, Taylor is sent on assignment to South Africa to discover the inspiration behind Aimee Amour, the DeBois estate's flagship wine. Mystery has enshrouded the story of the woman for whom the wine is named.

South African winegrower Armand DeBois's world is shattered when a car accident leaves him in a coma for three weeks, and his young wife dead. The road of recovery and mourning is dark, and Armand teeters between falling away from God and falling into His comforting arms.

When Armand and Taylor meet, questions arise for them both. While the country and the winegrower hold a strange attraction for Taylor, Armand struggles with the uncertainty of whether he's falling in love with his past or his future.

When his wife dies in childbirth, conservationist Simon Hartley pours his life into raising his daughter and his orphan elephants. He has no time, or desire, to fall in love again. Or so he thinks.

Wanting to escape English society and postpone an arranged marriage, Lady Abigail Chadwick heads to Africa for a year to teach the children of the Good Shepherd Orphanage. Upon her arrival she is left stranded at Livingstone airport…until a reluctant Simon comes to her rescue.

Now only fears born of his loss, and secrets of the life she's tried to leave behind, can stonewall their romance, budding in the heart of Africa.

Escaping his dangerous past, former British rock star Justin "The Phoenix" Taylor flees as far away from home as possible to Australia. A marked man with nothing left but his guitar and his talent, Justin is desperate to start over yet still live off the grid. Loneliness and the need to feel a connection to the London pastor who'd saved his life draw Justin to Ella's Barista Art Coffee Shop—the famous and trendy Melbourne establishment belonging to Pastor Jim Anderson's niece.

Intrigued by the bearded stranger who looks vaguely familiar, Ella Anderson wearies of serving him his regular flat white espresso every morning with no more than a greeting for conversation. Ella decides to discover his secrets, even if it requires coaxing him with her elaborate latte art creations. And muffins.

Justin gradually begins to open up to Ella but fears his past will collide with their future. When it does, Ella must decide whether they have a future at all.

1972. Every day in Belfast, Northern Ireland, holds risk, especially for the mayor's daughter. But Dr. Olivia O'Hare has a heart for people and chooses to work on the wrong side of a city where colors constantly clash. The orange and green of the Republicans pitted against the red and blue of those loyal to Britain. While they might share the common hue of white, it brings no peace.

Caught between the Republicans and Loyalists' conflict, blue-collar worker Ryann Doyle has to wonder if there's life before death. The answer seems to be a resounding, 'No'. His mother is dead, his father's a drunk, and his younger brother, Declan, is steeped in the Provisional IRA. Then he crosses paths with Olivia O'Hare.

After working four days straight, mopping up PIRA's latest act of terror,

Olivia is exhausted. All she wants is to go home and rest. But when she drives away from Royal Victoria Hospital, rest is the last thing Olivia gets.

When Declan kidnaps the Lord Mayor of Belfast's daughter, Ryann has to find a way to rescue the dark-haired beauty, though it means he must turn his back on his own flesh and blood for someone he just met.

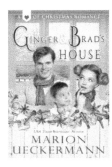 While Ginger Murphy completes her music studies, childhood sweetheart and neighbor, Brad O'Sullivan betrays her with the new girl next door. Heartbroken, Ginger escapes as far away as she can go—to Australia—for five long years. During this time, Brad's shotgun marriage fails. Besides his little boy, Jamie, one other thing in his life has turned out sweet and successful—his pastry business.

When her mother's diagnosed with heart failure, Ginger has no choice but to return to the green grass of Ireland. As a sought-after wedding flautist, she quickly establishes herself on home soil. Although she loves her profession, she fears she'll never be more than the entertainment at these joyous occasions. And that she's doomed to bump into the wedding cake chef she tries to avoid. Brad broke her heart once. She won't give him a chance to do it again.

A gingerbread house contest at church to raise funds for the homeless has Ginger competing with Brad. Both are determined to win—Ginger the contest, Brad her heart. But when a dear old saint challenges that the Good Book says the first shall be last, and the last first, Ginger has to decide whether to back down from contending with Brad and embrace the true meaning of Christmas—peace on earth, good will to all men. Even the Irishman she'd love to hate.

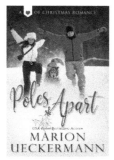

Writer's block and a looming Christmas novel deadline have romance novelist, Sarah Jones, heading for the other side of the world on a whim.

Niklas Toivonen offers cozy Lapland accommodation, but when his aging father falls ill, Niklas is called upon to step into his father's work clothes to make children happy. Red is quite his color.

Fresh off the airplane, a visit to Santa sets Sarah's muse into overdrive. The man in red is not only entertaining, he's young—with gorgeous blue eyes. Much like her new landlord's, she discovers. Santa and Niklas quickly become objects of research—for her novel, and her curiosity.

Though she's written countless happily-ever-afters, Sarah doubts she'll ever enjoy her own. Niklas must find a way to show her how to leave the pain of her past behind, so she can find love and faith once more.

Opera singer, Skye Hunter, returns to the land of her birth as leading lady in Phantom of the Opera. This is her first trip back to bonnie Scotland since her mother whisked her away to Australia after Skye's father died sixteen years ago.

When Skye decides to have dinner at McGuire's, she's not going there only for Mary McGuire's shepherd's pie. Her first and only love, Callum McGuire, still plays his guitar and sings at the family-owned tavern.

Callum has never stopped loving Skye. Desperate to know if she's changed under her mother's influence, he keeps his real profession hidden. Would she want him if he was still a singer in a pub? But when Skye's worst nightmare comes true, Callum reveals his secret to save the woman he loves.

Can Skye and Callum rekindle what they lost, or will her mother threaten their future together once again?

"If women were meant to fly, the skies would be pink."

Those were the first words Anjelica Joergensen heard from renowned wingsuiter, Kyle Sheppard, when they joined an international team in Oslo to break the formation flying Guinness World Record. This wouldn't be the last blunder Kyle would make around the beautiful Norwegian.

The more Anjelica tries to avoid Kyle, the more the universe pushes them together. Despite their awkward start, she finds herself reluctantly attracted to the handsome New Zealander. But beneath his saintly exterior, is Kyle just another daredevil looking for the next big thrill?

Falling for another wingsuiter would only be another love doomed.

When a childhood sweetheart comes between them, Kyle makes a foolish agreement which jeopardizes the event and endangers his life, forcing Angelica to make a hard choice.

Is she the one who'll clip his wings?

Can he be the wind beneath hers?

Three weeks alone at a friend's summer cottage on a Finnish lake to fast and pray. That was Adam Carter's plan. But sometimes plans go awry.

On an impromptu trip to her family's secluded summer cottage, the last thing Eveliina Mikkola expected to find was a missionary from the other side of the world—in her sauna.

Determined to stay, Eveliina will do whatever it takes—from shortcrust pastry to shorts—to send the man of God packing. This island's too small for them both.

Adam Carter, however, is not about to leave.

Will he be able to resist her temptations?

Can she withstand his prayers?

 Their outdoor wedding planned for the middle of Africa's rainy summer, chances are it'll pour on Mirabelle Kelly's bridal parade—after all, she is marrying Noah Raines.

To make matters worse, the African Rain Queen, Modjadji, is invited to the wedding.

Mirabelle must shun her superstitions and place her faith in the One who really controls the weather.

Note: This short story is in the *Dancing up a Storm* anthology.

Printed in the USA
CPSIA information can be obtained
at www.ICGtesting.com
LVHW040847060424
776638LV00029B/344